New York, New York!

Other books by
Ann M. Martin

Ma and Pa Dracula
Yours Turly, Shirley
Ten Kids, No Pets
Slam Book
Just a Summer Romance
Missing Since Monday
With You and Without You
Me and Katie (the Pest)
Stage Fright
Inside Out
Bummer Summer

BABY-SITTERS LITTLE SISTER series
THE BABY-SITTERS CLUB series
(see back of the book for a complete listing)

New York, New York!

Ann M. Martin

Interior illustrations by Henry R. Martin

SCHOLASTIC INC.
New York Toronto London Auckland Sydney

Cover art by Hodges Soileau

ISBN 0-590-43576-0

12 11 10 9 8 7 6 5 4 3 2 1 1 2 3 4 5 6/9

Printed in the U.S.A. 40

First Scholastic printing, June 1991

This Super Special
is for a super special friend,
Kendra Hines,
with love from BSC

New York, New York!

Well, its finally hapened. I made a decisoin. I decided to do something serius about my art. I'am not braging but I know Im a good artist. Ive been taking art lesons for as long as I can remerber. I love to draw, paint, make scluptures and even make jewlery. Some of my things have been on desplay in exibits and shows. I have won prizes. But I have never taken serious art clases, just clases at the arts center here in Stoneybrook Conneticut. Then guess waht. I read about a school in New York City. A art school! It is called a open school, whitch means you can take classes there whenever you whant for as long as you whant. And you can study with real, profesional artists like McKenzie Clarke or Nina Paryada. (In case you havnt noticed I'am not much of a speller, but I know I spelled those names wright becuase I looked them up.)

Anyway, I had a glorous school vacation coming up. My friends, the grils in the Baby-sitters Club (or the BSC), and I were realy looking forward for it.

Then I got my big idea. "Please, please, please can I go to New York City for two weeks?" I begged mom and dad. "I could take art lessins at the Fine Arts League of New York. They let you take clases whenever you want. I could maybe study with Nina or Mckenzie."

My parents looked confuzed at first. But they didnt ask who Nina and Mckenzie are. Insted they said, "Go to New York? For two weeks?"

I knew waht they were getting at. "I would not go by myself," I said indignintly. "Stacey is going to New York to visit her father." (Stacey is my best freind. Her parnets are divorced.) "I could stay at the McGills."

Mom and Dad were not crazy abot the idea. But then Mr. McGill called personilly and said he would be happy to have me stay with him and Stacey. So my parents said I could go. Just like that! They said that studing art would be a great thing to do on vacation. And then ... Mr. McGill said that any of Stacey's other friends wold be welcom to come to.

I gues you can figure out how the rest of the bsc felt wehn they heard my news. They were realy exited. Especially Mallory Pike. When she saw the infromation the Fine Arts League had sent me she begged her parents to let her go to the school too. (Mallory likes to draw. And she loves writing. Someday she whants to write and illistrate books for children.) The Pikes said yes and before I knew it, the whole BSC was going to go to New Yurk for two weeks. We could not believe it!

"You guys," I said to my friends, "will you help me out. I'am going to keep a diary of our trip, and Im going to illistrate it. Will you keep diaries too and let me use some of your notes? If you do, then my special diary will be a story about waht hapens to all of us."

My freinds were so excited they would have agreed to do almost anything, so they said yes quickly. Then they went on talking about waht they should pack for New York.

And waht they wanted to do there. Mary Anne Spier was the most excited of all. She really does ♥ New York. She knows tons about it, even tho she has only been there a few times. She has all these guidbooks. She talks like a guidbook too. And for days she went arond singing, "New York, New York! A wonderful town. The Bronx is --"

"I don't think those lyricks are quite right," Stacey would interrupt. "Doesn't the song go: New York, New York! A he--"

Then Mary Anne would cut her off. "I'll sing my own version," she would say. Then she would start over. "New York, New York! A wonderful town. The Bronx is up and the Battery's down."

"The batterys are down?" I siad.

"Never mind," answerd Mary Anne.

And I didnt. Who could mind? My freinds and I were about to set off for two wonderful weeks in . . . the big Apple!

Claudia

Wednesday

Oh, my lord I cant beleive it! My teacher at the Fine Arts League will be McKenzie Clarke. I had hardly dared to think that might happen. But it did. When we arrived in New York, Mal and I would be taking clases with McKenzie Clarke. With THE McKenzie Clarke. With HIM. We havnt even started packing yet but in my mind I'am already in New york studing with a famouse artist. I wonder if he's married....

Claudia

By now some of you might be wondering a few things. You might be wondering what the Baby-sitters Club is. You might be wondering who the rest of my friends are. Oh, and I guess you might be wondering who *I* am.

Well, I'll start with that last part. I am Claudia Kishi. I'm thirteen years old and I'm an eighth-grader at Stoneybrook Middle School. So are my friends Stacey McGill, Mary Anne Spier, Kristy Thomas, and Dawn Schafer. Mallory Pike and Jessi (short for Jessica) Ramsey, are sixth-graders at SMS. (They're best friends.) And we are the main members of the BSC. Kristy Thomas founded the club. It was her idea to get together a group of her friends who like to baby-sit, and for us to hold meetings three times a week. While we're meeting (in my room — club headquarters), parents call and line up sitters for their kids. They know they're bound to find a sitter, since when they phone during a meeting they reach all seven of us. Our club has turned into a business, and it's very successful. It's fun, too. My friends and I *love* children, and we've had some interesting sitting adventures. Plus, we've had lots of good times together as a club. We've had sleepovers and pizza parties, studied together, gone shopping together, and taken trips together.

Now we would soon be off on another trip. To New York City. The home of museums, theaters, the Hard Rock Cafe, Bloomingdale's, the Statue of Liberty, the Empire State Building, Macy's, South Street Seaport, Lord and Taylor, Madison Square Garden, Saks Fifth Avenue, and HIM. McKenzie Clarke.

Even though it was only Wednesday, and the BSC members wouldn't be leaving on their wonderful two-week trip until Saturday, I had started packing. My suitcase was open on my bed. And already it was as cluttered and messy as my room usually is. Except that my room is cluttered with art supplies — paper, paints, pastels, canvases, an easel, and boxes of "stuff."

My mother says I am a pack rat. So what? Pack rats are probably very nice animals. And I bet they're prepared for anything. I know I am.

Anyway, my suitcase was cluttered with about three years' worth of clothing, and a whole pile of things that I couldn't decide whether to pack. Would I need suntan lotion and three bathing suits? Probably not. I took them out and dropped them on the floor. Then

I began weeding out articles of clothing, entire outfits. I wondered if my other friends were having as hard a time packing as I was. We had all decided to pack that afternoon. Then we were going to ask Stacey her opinion of the things we were bringing. (Stacey is a New York expert, since she grew up there.) We figured that if Stacey said we'd made any horrible packing boo-boos, we'd have almost three days to straighten them out before we left on our trip.

Stacey, I knew, would be methodically placing just the right things in her suitcase. Since she's a little wild, her clothing would be sophisticated and extremely chilly. (My friends and I now say that something is "chilly" when it's really, really cool.) Stacey would be packing black leggings (some with stirrups on the feet, some without) and baggy black and white and red tops. She would probably pack or wear her black cowboy boots. Stacey and I both look good in black and white. Stace's hair is blonde and curly, usually as the result of a perm (the curliness, I mean; not its color). Her eyes are a deep blue, and she has neat dimples when she smiles. Stacey wears very chilly jewelry (so do I; we both have pierced ears), and she loves to do things that make herself look a little unusual. She might sprinkle glitter in her hair, or paint her nails silver.

Stacey lived in New York until she was twelve. She lived there with her mom and dad. (She has no sisters or brothers.) Then, just before seventh grade started, the McGills moved here. Mr. McGill's company had transferred him to their offices in Stamford, which is not far from Stoneybrook. The McGills had been in Connecticut for only about a year, when Mr. McGill was transferred *back* to New York. (I cried a *lot* when my new best friend moved away.) But once they were in the city again, Mr. and Mrs. McGill began arguing and fighting. They decided to get a divorce. And Stacey's mom decided to move back to Connecticut, while Mr. McGill stayed in New York with his job. Now Stacey lives in Stoneybrook again, but she visits her dad pretty often.

Sound like a tough life? Well, that's not all. Stacey has a disease called diabetes. She happens to have a severe form of it, and she's been pretty sick a few times. (Stacey is well acquainted with hospitals.) She can control her diabetes partly by sticking to a strict, calorie-counting diet, which allows her no candy or desserts. Poor thing. I, personally, am addicted to candy and junk food. Stacey also has to give herself injections (ew!) of something called insulin. I hope she stays healthy. I don't want her to land in the hospital again.

I imagined Kristy packing. Even though Kristy lives in a mansion with her mom and her millionaire stepfather, she was probably just tossing jeans and turtleneck shirts or T-shirts into a duffel bag. Kristy has never been one to dress up, and she has not always been rich. Until the summer before eighth grade, Kristy lived right across the street from me in a little house with her mom and her three brothers. (Mr. Thomas walked out on his family when Kristy was about six.) But then Mrs. Thomas married Watson the millionaire. Watson moved the Thomases across town to his mansion. So now Kristy lives in this ritzy house with her new family, which includes (aside from her mother and brothers) her adopted sister, Emily; her grandmother; her stepbrother and stepsister (only sometimes); and a cat, a dog, and some fish.

Kristy's life may have changed, but her taste hasn't. She's still a tomboy who loves sports and animals and who hates to get dressed up. When Stacey inspects Kristy's suitcase, she's going to have to do some fast talking to convince Kristy to add so much as a skirt to her pile of jeans. Oh, well. Kristy may be a little less mature than some of us, but we love her anyway.

Next I imagined Dawn packing. When I thought of her, I could picture Mary Anne packing in the next bedroom. Why are Dawn Schafer and Mary Anne Spier in the same house? Because they're stepsisters, that's why. See, Mary Anne's mom died when Mary Anne was just a baby. So she grew up with her father, who was sort of strict with her. Her life was lonely, I think. Thank goodness she used to live next door to Kristy. Kristy is one of her two best friends. (Her other best friend is Dawn.) Anyway, when Stacey, Mary Anne, Kristy, and I were about halfway through seventh grade, Dawn, her mom, and her younger brother, Jeff, moved to Stoneybrook from California. Dawn's parents were getting divorced, and her mom had grown up in Stoneybrook. Dawn and Mary Anne became friends pretty quickly. But they never imagined they'd become *stepsisters*. It all started when they discovered that Mary Anne's father and Dawn's mother had been high-school sweethearts years ago. Boy, were my friends surprised! But they were sneaky, too. They found ways to get their parents together every now and then, and before they knew it, Mr. Spier and Mrs. Schafer were dating (again). Now they're married. Mary Anne, her dad, and her kitten, Tigger, moved into the Schafers' farmhouse, where they live happily. Oh, except for the fact that Jeff isn't with them anymore. Jeff never adjusted to life in Connecticut, so he moved back to California and his dad even before Dawn and Mary Anne became stepsisters.

Let me see. Dawn, who's individualistic and pretty self-confident, would be packing her own personal style of clothes, which the rest of us think of as "California casual." (In my opinion, Dawn would look good in anything. She's gorgeous, with long, silky blonde hair, piercing blue eyes, and just enough freckles to be interesting.) Mary Anne, who looks something like Kristy — they're both on the short side, and have brown eyes and brown hair — will be packing her very different wardrobe. Mary Anne used to have to wear clothes her father picked out for her. She looked like a first-grader. Now she wears much chillier clothes.

Hmm. At the Pikes', Mallory was probably tripping over her seven younger brothers and sisters and packing the trendiest stuff she could find. Unfortunately, Mr. and Mrs. Pike don't allow Mal to dress very fashionably. They're not strict parents, but Mal *is* only eleven. So far, they have allowed her to get her ears pierced. They have *not* allowed her to switch her glasses for contacts, to have her braces taken off early, to have her curly red hair straightened, or to wear just about anything that Stacey or I get to wear. She manages not to look like a first-grader, though. She spends most of her baby-sitting money on any clothes or jewelry she thinks she can get away with wearing. (She spends the rest of her money on journals, and on materials for drawing and sketching, and on books. Mallory is a big writer and a big reader. She especially likes horse stories.)

Jessi Ramsey likes to read, too, but her true love is ballet. Jessi is a very talented dancer. She takes special classes at a school in Stamford, and she has danced onstage before hundreds of people. She would probably pack a leotard and her toe shoes. (She likes to exercise even when she's on vacation.) Otherwise, she would pack stuff pretty similar to Mallory's. Her parents feel the same way about clothes that the Pikes do. This is interesting, since the Pikes and the Ramseys are pretty dissimilar. The Pikes are white, the Ramseys are black. There are eight Pike kids, but just three Ramsey kids. The Pikes have lived in Stoneybrook since before Mal was born. The Ramseys moved here (right into Stacey's old house!) at the beginning of the school year. I guess the parents of eleven-year-olds are sort of the same everywhere.

And what was left in *my* suitcase after I'd removed that three years' worth of clothing? Outfits like Stacey's, only wilder, if you can believe it. I would say that, like Stacey, I'm pretty sophisticated, but I may be the chilliest dresser in the BSC. That's because I *like* to look different from other people. I make a lot of my own jewelry — big, dangly earrings, papier-mâché bracelets and pins — and I'm always trying new ways to wear belts, layer my clothes, fix my hair. . . . I'm Japanese-American, and my hair is long and straight and black. It looks good when I pull it back with bright ribbons or combs or barrettes. And my eyes are dark and almond-shaped. I think I look exotic, especially with the right kind of makeup.

I stepped back and checked my suitcase. The floor around the bed was littered with discarded outfits, I *still* wasn't going to be able to close the suitcase, and I hadn't even packed my art materials yet. I had to bring them along if I was going to study with HIM.

Oh, well. I'd just borrow another suitcase from my sister.

Kristy

Saturday

My friends and I left for New York City today. I've been there before, but not for two whole weeks. What a great vacation this was going to be. Maybe I would get to see a Mets game. I had already checked to see if the dog show would be going on at Madison Square Garden. It wouldn't. I had missed it. But I didn't care. I wanted to go sightseeing. I wanted to buy lots of New York souvenirs. I wanted to feel grown-up and important.

Kristy

It was time to say good-bye. I have never liked that very much. Not because it's sad or because maybe I'll never again see the people I'm saying good-bye to. (Mary Anne is always sure of that; she thinks some disaster will strike.) It's just that people get so mushy when they're saying good-bye. Also, my family is pretty big, so we make a spectacle of ourselves at train stations or airports.

These are the people who came to the train station to see me off on the day we left for New York: Mom, my stepfather, my grandmother Nannie, Charlie and Sam (my big brothers), David Michael (my little brother), Karen and Andrew (my stepsister and stepbrother), Emily Michelle (my adopted sister), and our dog, Shannon. I'm surprised the cat and the goldfish didn't come, too.

At least this time I didn't feel as conspicuous as usual. That's because eventually *all* the members of *each* of my friends' families showed up. You can imagine what the Pike crowd looked like. Before they arrived, though, I had to deal with my family myself. Mom had insisted that we leave for the station a half an hour before the train to New York was due in. The station is exactly four minutes from our house. That left us with twenty-six minutes to kill — and an audience of about fifteen people to watch us kill the time.

I hope they were entertained. We did our best to put on a show for them.

Emily, who is two and a half, used my suitcase and backpack as her own personal jungle gym. She kept trying to stand on top of the suitcase (when *it* was standing up). And Mom kept saying, "Be careful, Emily. Emily, be *care*ful."

Then there was Karen, who's seven, jumping all around, singing, "New York, New York! A wonderful town. The Bronx is up and the Battery's down!" Mary Anne had baby-sat for her and Andrew two days before.

Meanwhile, Andrew (who's almost five) and David Michael (who's going on eight) found one of the rattly baggage carts.

"Cool!" exclaimed David Michael.

"Give me a ride!" said Andrew, scrambling on.

Nannie saw them. "David Michael! Andrew! That isn't a toy!" she called. (Pause.) "David Michael, come back here! Andrew, please get off."

I had the feeling that the people around us were quickly learning our names.

"Kristy, will you buy me something in New York?" asked Karen loudly.

"Me, too?" cried Andrew and David Michael, abandoning the baggage cart.

"Potty!" exclaimed Emily Michelle.

"I'll take her," said Mom.

Luckily, Mallory and her family arrived then, and the people at the station found them more interesting than my family. (Anyway, there were fewer of us at that point. David Michael, Andrew, and Karen had all followed Mom to the bathrooms, and Charlie had taken Shannon for a quick walk in the parking lot.) Here's the thing about the Pikes: Three of the boys are ten-year-old identical triplets. They don't dress in matching outfits, but their faces are *exactly* the same. There's no mistaking that they're triplets.

"Hi, Mal!" I called.

"Hi!" she replied. "Guess what. I had to *pay* Jordan to carry my suitcase." Mallory pointed to one of the triplets.

"Well, you offered," said Jordan.

"I did not. You said, 'Want me to carry your suitcase?' and I said, 'Sure,' and you said, 'Okay, that'll be fifty cents.' "

I giggled. "Hey, here come Mary Anne and Dawn."

Mallory clapped her hand over her mouth. "I don't believe it. Mary Anne brought Tigger with her!" Tigger was mewing pitifully inside his carrier.

"Well, now I don't feel so bad," I said. "Everyone's looking at Tigger."

Ten minutes later, the rest of the BSC had reached the train station. There were Jessi, her parents, her Aunt Cecelia, and her younger sister and baby brother. There were Claudia, her sister, and her mom and dad. And there were Stacey and her mom.

My friends and I huddled together, away from our families.

"Do you think anyone knows we belong with them?" asked Claudia, indicating the knot of anxious parents, and the kids who were running around.

"I'm afraid so," I replied. "They even know the names of my brothers and sisters. We're hard to miss."

Claud sighed.

Then Dawn spoke up. "This morning my mom asked Mary Anne and me if we *really* wanted to go to New York for two weeks. She said if we stayed here she'd take us on a shopping spree. I told her that New York was going to be one big spree all by itself, didn't I, Mary Anne? . . . Mary Anne?"

Mary Anne had opened a booklet about New York and was gazing at it intently. "You know," she began, "if all the coffee shops in New York City were placed side by side, I bet they would — "

Dawn groaned, and Mary Anne stopped talking. She went right back to the book, though, and immediately became lost in it again.

"Uh-oh," I whispered.

"What?" asked Jessi.

"Look." I pointed to our parents. They had gathered in a pack under the sign that read: NEW YORK-BOUND TRAINS.

"Ooh," breathed Jessi. "That doesn't look good. You don't think they'll suddenly decide not to let us go, do you?"

"They might," Mal replied darkly.

"I'll take care of them," announced Stacey. She marched over to the parents. The rest of us followed her uncertainly.

When the grown-ups saw us coming, they stopped talking — which only proved that they *had* been talking about us.

"So," said Stacey, "my dad's apartment is

ready for us. Well, for some of us." (Mr. McGill's apartment isn't big enough to be overtaken by seven extra people for two weeks, so only Stacey and two others were going to stay with him. The rest of us would stay on the other side of town with Laine Cummings and her family. Laine is an old friend of Stacey's, and she and her parents live in a *huge* apartment.) "Dad even had the apartment professionally cleaned," Stacey went on. "Exterminated, too."

"Ex*ter*minated?" repeated Mrs. Ramsey. "You mean it has roaches?" She looked as if she were about to cry.

"No, giant sewer rats," I whispered, but Dawn poked me in the ribs.

"Well, yes," Stacey said to Mrs. Ramsey. "But, see, the important thing is that now they're gone."

"Besides," spoke up Mrs. McGill, who was the only sane-looking adult on the platform, "almost every apartment in New York has roaches. They're like flies or ants in most — "

"They carry disease," murmured Nannie, shuddering.

Stacey and her mom exchanged a Look.

The loudspeaker was turned on then, and

a tinny voice announced, "The train bound for New York is approaching the station. Two minutes to boarding time."

My mother burst into tears.

Dawn's mother said, "I hope all the dishes and pots and pans were washed after those exterminators sprayed their poison around."

Mrs. Ramsey hugged Jessi protectively.

Emily fell off my suitcase and skinned her knee.

In the midst of her tears, I spied the headlight on our train, and soon the engine was roaring into the station. "Here we go!" I cried, but I was caught first in an embrace by Nannie, then by Mom, and then by Watson. All around me, the other parents were hugging their kids. Half of the parents were crying. (None of my friends was. Although Mary Anne was poking her fingers into the cat carrier, and saying, " 'Bye, Tiggy-Tiggy-Tiggy.")

"Okay, Watson, I gotta go," I said, pulling away. I stepped onto the train, followed by Claudia, Jessi, Mary Anne, Mallory, and Dawn. We struggled with our luggage until I noticed that Stacey hadn't boarded the train yet. She was still outside, saying things like, "I *pro*mise I won't let them ride the subway alone," and, "I don't think anyone would *want* to buy a hot dog from a street vendor."

"I would," said Claudia, but luckily her parents didn't hear her.

"Come *on,* Stacey!" I cried. "The train's going to leave without you." I made a grab for her just as the doors started to close.

When Stacey was safely on board, the seven of us waved and called, "Good-bye! Good-bye!" Then we found an almost empty car. This was a good thing, since we and our luggage took up fifteen seats.

"We made it!" I said, as if we'd just escaped from prison.

"Okay, lunchtime," was Claudia's reply.

"*Lunch*time? It's only ten o'clock," Mary Anne informed her.

"Well, I'm hungry."

The rest of us decided we were, too, so we ate the snacks we'd brought along. Then Mary Anne returned to the stack of maps and guidebooks she brings along on every trip we take.

"Does anyone else have a sense of *déjà vu*?" I asked, glancing at Mary Anne.

"Me!" cried Claudia and Dawn, who'd been with Mary Anne and me when we'd visited Stacey for a weekend during the time she was back in New York.

"What could she possibly *not* know about New York by now?" I wondered aloud.

"That there's a Hall of Chinese History at some place called the Bowery," Mary Anne replied.

I shook my head. Then I gazed out the window.

An hour or so later, a deep voice was saying, "All out for New York. This is Grand Central Station. Last stop!"

The train jerked to a halt.

"Ooh, we're *here*," whispered Mary Anne.

Somehow we managed to get all of our stuff — suitcases, backpacks, duffel bags, tote bags, pocketbooks, and cameras — off of the train. Then we followed Stacey through thick, stuffy air and into the crowded station.

"Dad!" Stacey shouted, waving her hand.

I looked up and saw Mr. McGill running toward us.

Mary Anne

Saturday

I can't believe it. We've only been in New York for a few hours, and already Stacey and I have a baby-sitting job! Pretty amazing. It's sort of a dream job, since the parents are hiring us not just to baby-sit, but to show their two little kids around the city. (The family is visiting from England. The parents are here on political business.) This is quite an arrangement. I'm actually going to get paid to sightsee all over New York. I would have gone sightseeing anyway, but now I don't have to

Mary Anne

spend my own money. I can save it up for something really chilly. Like a suitcase full of New York souvenirs. Or better yet, a charm bracelet with the Statue of Liberty, the Empire State Building, and other things hanging from it. Or maybe a huge book of photos of New York. Or even...

"Oof. That weighs a ton, honey. What did you pack? Anvils?" Mr. McGill said to Stacey as he lugged her suitcase through the door to his apartment. He stood for a moment, just holding it. Finally he said, "I'm afraid to put it down. I'm afraid it will go through the floor and land on the Magnesis' dining room table. Or worse, on one of the Magnesis."

I laughed, but Stacey barely heard her father. She was standing at a window, breathing in deeply. "Mmm," she said contentedly. "I can almost smell — "

"New Jersey?" suggested Kristy.

"No, Bloomingdale's. Dad, I am forever

grateful to you for getting an apartment within walking distance of Bloomingdale's."

We were all laughing by then. Mr. McGill finally put the suitcase down and told us to put our things down, too. We did, heaving sighs of relief.

"Now, who's staying where?" asked Stacey's father.

"Well, I'm staying here, of course," replied Stace.

"Me, too," said Claud. (Best friends stick together.)

"I don't mind going to Laine's," spoke up Kristy.

"Neither do I," I said.

"Neither do I," said both Jessi and Mallory.

Dawn was the only one who didn't say anything, and I realized she'd been sort of quiet ever since we'd reached Grand Central, and especially ever since an ambulance had gone screaming by the cab we were riding in, and then a second cab had almost broadsided us and our driver had leaned out of his window and screamed something unrepeatable at the top of his lungs.

"Welcome to New York," Stacey had whispered.

I'd laughed, but Dawn had sat next to me like a statue.

Now Stacey spoke up. "Dawn, why don't you stay here with Claud and me? I don't think we can ask the Cummingses to take *five* houseguests for two weeks."

So it was settled. Dawn looked extremely relieved at the idea of staying where she was. But she looked less relieved when Stacey had gone on to say, "Okay, Dawn, you and Claud dump your stuff in my room. Then we'll go over to Laine's with everyone else."

A few minutes later we were out on the street again, hailing cabs and then stuffing people and luggage inside them and heading to the Upper West Side. The Cummingses live in one of the most famous buildings in all of New York City. It's called the Dakota, and the apartments in it are huge and expensive. I think Laine's parents are millionaires. (I was beside myself with the thought of actually staying in the Dakota for two whole weeks. The old movie *Rosemary's Baby* was filmed there. Famous people live there. Famous people have *died* there, too.)

I hoped I was dressed properly for the Dakota. Stacey had done a suitcase-check in Sto-

The Dakota, where Laine lives

neybrook and told me that I had packed well. Still . . .

I felt better, though, when Stacey had led us to Laine's apartment. Laine had let us in, and I had found both Mr. and Mrs. Cummings dressed in jeans, and Laine dressed in a black-and-white Stacey-like outfit.

"Hi!" cried Laine, and then the introductions and the reminders of who was who began. Jessi and Mal had met Laine before but hadn't met her parents. The rest of us knew Laine pretty well but her parents less well.

I was glad when the Cummingses seemed to have gotten our names straightened out and Laine said, "Come on back to the bedrooms, you guys." (I hated for our luggage to junk up the grand living room.)

We picked up our belongings and followed Laine down a hallway. "Here's my room," she announced. I peeked in and saw a pair of twin beds. "There's a trundle bed underneath one," Laine informed us, "and there are two more beds in the guest room."

With no arguing at all, it was decided that Kristy and I would stay in Laine's room, since we knew her better than Jessi and Mal did, and that Jessi and Mal would sleep in the guest room.

Mary Anne

"Gosh, this apartment is *beau*tiful," I could hear Mallory say as we were stowing our stuff in out-of-the-way places.

"Yeah, look out the window," Jessi replied. "Look at all those trees and the grass. Who says New York is just a mass of buildings?"

"That's Central Park!" I called from Laine's room. I thought I heard someone say something about a "talking guidebook," but I wasn't sure. Anyway, at that moment the doorbell rang. (Dawn screamed.)

"Who's that, Mom?" yelled Laine.

"Probably the Harringtons," was the reply.

"Oh." Laine turned to Kristy and Dawn and me. "The Harringtons are going to be staying in the Baickers' apartment upstairs. Mr. and Mrs. Baicker are friends of my parents. They had planned a trip to England and Mrs. Baicker knew that her cousins, the Harringtons, were going to be traveling over *here*, so they just traded apartments with the Harringtons. Isn't that cool?"

"Chilly," replied Kristy.

Laine grinned. "Let's go meet them. I think Mom said the Harringtons have kids. I wonder if they brought them along."

The Harringtons did have kids. When Laine and I and the members of the BSC trooped back into the living room, we saw Mr. and Mrs. Cummings talking to a couple — and a little boy and girl standing around, looking bored.

Introductions started all over again. In the middle of everything, Mr. Harrington rested his hand on the boy's head and said, "This is Alistaire."

Alistaire smiled politely. "Hullo," he said, "I'm seven."

"And this is Rowena," Mr. Harrington went on, placing his hand on the girl's head.

"I'm this many." Rowena held up four fingers.

Everyone smiled. I was absolutely enchanted. Rowena and Alistaire looked up at the adults from under perfectly combed, dark brown bangs. Their eyes were round and green. And they were dressed like . . . well, certainly not like many kids I know. Alistaire was wearing a white sailor suit with navy blue trim, white knee socks, and black shoes that buckled at the sides. They looked a little like Mary Janes, only they weren't shiny. And Rowena was wearing a white sailor dress, similar to Alistaire's suit, white tights, red Mary Janes, and a red hat. I don't remember the last time I saw a child wearing a hat that wasn't dripping with melted snow and smelling of wet wool. Perched on Rowena's head was a round straw hat, held in place by an elastic band under her chin. Red ribbons trailed from the back of the hat.

"We're visiting America for two weeks," Alistaire announced proudly. "Only Mummy and Daddy have to work."

It turned out that both Mr. and Mrs. Harrington were dignitaries. Or maybe diplomats. I'm not sure. They had something to do with the government, though, and apparently they were very important and extremely wealthy.

"We're lucky to have found a housekeeper while we're staying here," said Mrs. Harrington, "but we would really rather that the children weren't cooped up all day while we're busy. We'd like them to see New York. And anyway, we can't expect the housekeeper to be a nanny, too."

"In fact," added Mr. Harrington, "we were wondering if you" (he meant Laine's parents) "would know where we might find someone who could not only entertain Rowena and Alistaire, but who could show them New York. Take them to the zoo, go sightseeing — "

"Go to the big toy store!" exclaimed Rowena.

"FAO Schwarz?" said Stacey. "Oh, that's a neat place."

"Yes, Rowena has been asking to go to FAO Schwarz, and Alistaire would like to see the dinosaurs in the Museum of Natural History."

"The dinosaur *skeletons*," Alistaire corrected his father. "Not dinosaurs."

"Right," agreed Mr. Harrington cheerfully. He turned back to the Cummingses. "Do you know a good nanny service?" he asked.

Well, of course by now my friends and I were looking at each other excitedly. *We* would be perfect tour guides. And we know how to entertain kids. But did we dare suggest that? Laine took care of the problem for us.

"My friends are baby-sitters," she announced. Then she told the Harringtons about the BSC. They seemed impressed.

Mr. and Mrs. Harrington spoke briefly in the kitchen. When they returned, Mrs. Harrington said, "If you're interested, we would like to engage two of you to watch the children and to show them around the city." Then she added how much we would be paid, and the seven BSC members nearly fainted.

Even so, when *we* stepped into the kitchen to discuss the offer, not everyone jumped at it. Claudia and Mal couldn't take it because of their art classes. Jessi and Kristy wanted to sightsee, but not necessarily with kids. They both do their share of baby-sitting for their brothers and sisters, and they wanted a break from that while they were on vacation. Dawn never opened her mouth, but that turned out to be okay because Stacey said, "If you guys wouldn't mind, I'd kind of like the job. I know tons about New York." So *I* said, "I'll do the job with you, Stace. I can't believe the Harringtons are actually going to pay me to do one of the things I love the most — be a tourist!"

"Is this okay with the rest of you?" asked Stacey. "I don't want you to think I'm abandoning you. Anyway, Laine will be around."

"It's fine," chorused Claud, Jessi, Kristy, and Mal.

"Dawn?" I asked. She was sitting at the table, looking miserable. "Hey, are you feeling all right?"

"Sure," Dawn answered quickly. "Go ahead and tell the Harringtons they've got two experienced nannies for the next couple of weeks."

"Okay," I said, but I glanced at Stacey, because Dawn wasn't convincing me that she was happy with the arrangement.

Stacey just shrugged.

"Okay," said Kristy, taking charge (which she was born to do). "Let's go give the Harringtons the good news."

So we did. Mr. and Mrs. Harrington asked us to begin the next day.

Dawn

Saturday

Ever since my friends and I started talking about this trip to New York, I've felt a little funny. I tried to tell myself that I was just nervous, but as soon as our train entered that dark tunnel into Grand Central, I knew I was wrong.

I wasn't excited. I was scared to death.

Dawn

What on earth had I been thinking? The *last* time I visited New York (I mean, apart from day trips we'd taken to the hospital when Stacey was sick) I'd been scared to death. I don't know why I'd thought this time would be different. You know what's wrong? I keep remembering all those horror stories I read about crime and danger in New York City. Stacey says that's not fair. She says we can find crime and danger *any*where, even way out in the country (thanks a lot, Stace), but that New York has a bad reputation.

Well, I'm sorry. Maybe good old NYC wouldn't have such a bad reputation if so many awful things didn't go on there . . . and if newspaper reporters didn't eat up each grisly story as if it were a piece of candy. I just couldn't help reading news about New York for a few days before we left on our trip. I had to know what was going on in the city. And what did I read about? Robberies, snipers, muggings, bank holdups, that's what.

"Not fair!" exclaimed Stacey. "Didn't you read about any of the culture? The museums or the theater or street fairs — "

"There *was* an article about a street fair," I interrupted her. "It said how this gang of pickpockets ripped off *fifty-nine* people. They're just like the Artful Dodger in *Oliver Twist*. They can take a wallet out of your pocket, or even a watch off your wrist, without your feeling it."

Stacey sighed. "I'm not going to argue with you, Dawn. I'll just ask you this. Did *any*thing bad happen the first time you visited me in New York?"

I grinned. "We all got into a huge argument."

"How about when you visited me when I was in the hospital?" (Not long ago, Stacey was at her dad's for a weekend and got really sick with her diabetes and wound up in the hospital. That's when the rest of us came to visit her.)

"Nothing happened," I admitted.

"Okay, then," said Stace, as if she had solved all my problems.

"But something *could* happen. Anytime. Anywhere."

"You mean like something could fall off a building that's under construction and conk you on the head?" Kristy asked.

"Let's stay away from scaffolding and construction," I said.

Stacey had given Kristy a Very Mean Look.

Anyway, I was pretty proud of myself when I got on the train in Stoneybrook without hysterics, and then actually enjoyed the ride — until we got to Grand Central. Mary Anne was chattering away about Little Italy and Chinatown, and I was getting excited. (At least, I thought I was.) The next thing I knew, we were in that dark tunnel. The tunnel makes New York seem like some other-worldly place that you reach by hurtling through space and time. Then you step off the train and into hordes and hordes of people — including police officers, and men and women sleeping on the floor or on benches in the waiting room. That's what *I* saw when we reached New York. Claudia saw every ice cream stand and every possible source of junk food. And Mary Anne kept thinking she saw movie stars.

As we made our way to the information booth, where we were supposed to meet Mr. McGill, I looked down at the floor. And that was when I spotted . . . a cockroach the size of a dollar bill.

"Aughh!" I screamed.

"Grab your pocketbooks!" cried Mary Anne.

"What's wrong?" asked Stacey.

"It's not my pocketbook, it's — it's *that*." I pointed. "That roach. It's the biggest one

I've ever seen. I am *not* walking by it."

"Dawn, get a grip," said Claud. "That's a candy wrapper." Leave it to Claud to identify a candy wrapper from ten feet away.

"Are you sure?" I was trembling.

"Is this enough proof?" asked Claud. She marched over to the roach and picked it up. "See? Three Musketeers. . . . Boy, I could do with a Three Musketeers bar right now."

We met Mr. McGill and emerged into the sunshine unscathed.

I drew in a sigh of relief. "Made it," I muttered, just as a *POW* rang out and reverberated off the buildings around us.

"Duck!" I shrieked. "It's a car bomb!"

I heard laughter next to me. "Dawn," said Claud, "would you relax? You're going to give me a coronary. And we've only been in New York for five minutes."

"Well, what *was* that?" I asked shakily.

Stacey pointed across the street. "Construction. Those workers just blasted something open. And they — "

"Aughh!" I screamed again.

"What now?" asked Mr. McGill, but he didn't sound impatient.

"Look! Look at that guy at the magazine stand."

"The guy with the glasses?" asked Jessi. Everyone was peering at the stand.

"No, not him. The one with his back to us," I said.

"What about him?" asked Mal.

"He is on New York's Ten Most Wanted list. I saw something about him on TV last week. He escaped from prison."

"How can you tell it's him?" wondered Kristy.

"I just can. See that cap he's wearing? It's — "

Just then the man turned around.

"It's a police officer's hat," Kristy finished triumphantly.

Sure enough, The guy was a policeman.

I decided to keep my mouth shut for awhile. And I did. I didn't comment on our taxi ride to Mr. McGill's apartment. I didn't say how relieved and surprised I was when every one of us and every piece of luggage was safely inside the apartment.

And I certainly didn't ask Stacey's father why his apartment wasn't protected by an alarm system.

Then came the time to decide who was going to stay at Mr. McGill's and who was going to travel across town to Laine's. I almost asked, "Does Laine's apartment have a burglar alarm?" But I didn't. I knew the Dakota had excellent security — guards and all — and that Mr. McGill's building didn't even have a doorman. But I was afraid to go out again. Besides, I wanted to stick with Stacey. I felt safer with her.

Wouldn't you know — just my luck — everyone (except me) wanted to go to Laine's to help Kristy, Mary Anne, Jessi, and Mallory settle in. I thought about asking Mr. McGill if he wouldn't mind a little company that afternoon, but before I could say anything, he announced that he needed to run errands. I quickly decided to go with my friends to the Cummingses.' We were probably safer in a pack.

Boy. It seemed that all during Saturday I would just start to feel sort of safe somewhere — and we'd leave. After my friends had unpacked their things at Laine's, we returned to Mr. McGill's apartment. We were there long enough to gulp down sodas (or in my case, orange juice with seltzer in it; I like to eat healthy), and then Mr. McGill took us out to dinner. The restaurant seemed reasonably safe, especially since I positioned myself against a wall, facing the door, and watched who came in and went out. But of course we couldn't stay there all night.

"How about more coffee?" I kept saying to Stacey's father.

After his third cup he smiled and said, "I'm going to float away. Stacey, do you want to signal the waiter for our check?" (Stacey just loves doing that. It's as if she and the waiter know a secret code.)

Ten minutes later we were outside again. And soon Stacey, her father, Claud, and I were back at Mr. McGill's.

"Where do you guys want to sleep?" asked Stacey. "There's a futon in my room that unrolls into a pretty comfortable . . . bed. Well, mattress. And the couch in the living room opens into a double bed."

"I'll take the futon," said Claud. I knew she thought that she was doing me a favor. But I didn't want to sleep alone in the living room.

"Oh, that's okay. *I'll* take the futon," I told her grandly.

"No, really. You sleep on the bed."

"Come on, guys, don't argue about it," spoke up Stacey.

So I ended up on the sofa bed. All alone in

New York City. Sleeping right next to a window that opened onto a fire escape.

When I had stayed in Stacey's other apartment — the one she and her parents lived in before the divorce — I hadn't been nearly as scared. That apartment had been in a nice, big doorman building, on a very high floor, with indoor fire stairs. There were no fire escapes at the windows, which in my opinion was a blessing. As far as I'm concerned, a fire escape is an open invitation to a burglar. It says, "Hey! Come on in. Crawl right through the window. Take our VCR and our CD player. Help yourself."

I glanced uneasily over my shoulder at the window. I nearly screamed. Was that a figure standing outside? No. Just a shadow.

Ker-thunk. What was *that?* I listened. I heard crashes and banging in the street below. I could hear everything: voices, car horns, sirens, a screech of brakes, a car alarm going off. The alarm didn't ring like most normal alarms. Instead, a mechanized voice growled over and over, "Burglar, burglar, burglar." (The crashes and banging turned out to be a garbage truck.)

What a dreadful night. I barely slept.

And guess what happened in the morning. My friends deserted me.

When breakfast was over, Stacey jumped up from the table and said, "Well, gotta go. Rowena and Alistaire are waiting."

Claud jumped up, too. "I'll ride over there with you. I think I'll see what Laine's up to today. Are the stores open on Sunday?"

Stacey giggled. "Some of them are. Shopping already?"

"I've only got two weeks — and a whole city full of stores. Besides, starting tomorrow, I'm going to be really busy with classes."

"What about you, Dawn?" asked Stacey.

I glanced at Mr. McGill. "Um, I don't know."

"I've got to put in a few hours at the office," said Stacey's father. (He's a workaholic.)

"So come to Laine's with us, Dawn," said Claud.

"Oh . . . that's all right. I think I'll stay put." I couldn't bear to go outside again.

In the end, I was left alone. But not for long. Kristy took pity on me. Around lunchtime she appeared at Mr. McGill's, saying, "Okay, Dawn. Here I am. Your personal babysitter."

Stacey

Sunday

Today was our first day as tour guides for Rowena and Alistaire Harrington. We had a great time. They said they wanted to see Central Park, so that's where Mary Anne and I took them. Rowena and Alistaire loved everything (I think)-- the zoo, the carousel, the Delacorte clock, and the statues, especially Alice in Wonderland.

Stacey

I just love waking up in New York City. I love the noise. I love the sound of dogs barking and the breeze rattling the venetian blinds. I love trucks rattling down the street, and children calling to each other and laughing. I'm not being sarcastic. I really do love these sounds. When I'm in Connecticut, I like the quiet. But when I visit New York, I appreciate the noise.

Swish, swish, swish. I opened my eyes just as a street cleaner whooshed by Dad's apartment building. I ran to the window. "Good morning, New York!" I called.

On the floor beside me, Claudia stirred. "Close the window," she mumbled.

"It's too hot. You'll melt," I told her. "Go back to sleep."

And she did. I tiptoed out of my bedroom, down the hallway, through the living room (where Dawn was sound asleep, even though she said later that she hadn't slept a wink because of the fire escape), and into the kitchen.

"Morning, Dad," I said.

His face lit up. "Morning, Boontsie."

"Ugh. Dad, I'm much too old for that baby name." But I gave my father a hug. "How long have you been up?" I asked him.

"Just long enough to make coffee," he answered.

Dad and I sat down at the little table in the kitchen.

"This is nice," I said.

"What is?"

"This." I gestured around the room. "Everything. It's early, we're the only ones up, the coffee smells great. . . . We can have a private visit now."

Dad smiled. "What are you and your friends up to today?"

"I'm not sure about everyone else, but Mary Anne and I are going to take care of Alistaire and Rowena."

"So you'll be busy most of the day?"

"Probably. Why?"

"I thought I'd go to the office for a few hours."

"Again? On *Sun*day? Dad, can't you take some time off? You work too hard." Dad was pouring himself a cup of coffee, and I was slicing a bagel.

"I only went in for a few hours yesterday," he replied. "I need to make up for that."

"But yesterday was Saturday. Most people don't go to work *then*."

"I do."

"Would you go if I didn't have any plans today?"

"Of course not."

Well, that was something. But I had the vague feeling that Dad was glad I had plans so he wouldn't have to entertain me. I sighed. I think this must have been one of the problems between my parents. Now I understood how my mother had felt when she was married to Dad.

I knew Dad loved me, though, and that in the end I (not his work) came first. He'd shown me that the last time I was in the hospital. So I set aside my worries and got ready for my first job with the Harrington children.

"What are you going to wear?" Claud asked me later, as she and Dawn and I were getting dressed in my bedroom.

"For a day in the city with two little kids? My grubbies."

Claud laughed. "I didn't know you owned grubbies. Besides, do you really think Rowena and Alistaire will be dressed in grubbies?"

Good point. "No," I admitted, and opted for casual clothes, something between grubbies and matching, spotless sailor outfits.

Not much later, Claudia and I headed out

of Dad's apartment, reluctantly leaving Dawn behind. After my father left, Dawn would be on her own.

"What's she going to do all day?" Claudia wondered.

I shrugged. "She's got Laine's phone number. She can reach you guys if she decides to venture outside."

"Hullo! Hullo!" called Alistaire.

Mary Anne and I were standing in the foyer of the Harringtons' borrowed apartment. The housekeeper had let us in, and now Alistaire was running toward us, followed closely by Rowena. Once again, the kids were pretty dressed up, but I was relieved to see that at least they weren't wearing white. White is not the most practical color for New York, especially if you are four or seven.

"Good morning, Stacey. Good morning, Mary Anne." Mrs. Harrington joined us in the foyer. Talk about dressed up. What were she and her husband *doing?* They'd said they had to work.

Mrs. Harrington smiled. I must have been gaping at her outfit. "Lots of events today," she said. "Since we're here for just two weeks, our schedule is quite full. We may be able to spend some time with the children next week, though. For now — show them the city. They're very excited."

"I read about New York in a book," said Alistaire. "People call it the Big Apple. I want to see the tall buildings."

"I want to see the apple," said Rowena, and everyone tried not to laugh.

Mrs. Harrington handed me a wad of bills. "For expenses," she said. "I know Rowena and Alistaire will have much more fun with you two than with some stuffy grown-up." She smiled. "Don't give them *too* many sweets," she warned. "But show them the city the way a child would want to see it."

Mary Anne and I grinned.

"No problem," I said. "I grew up here."

"And I know *all* about New York," added Mary Anne.

"All right, then. Can you bring the children back by four o'clock?" (Mary Anne and I nodded.) "Lovely." Mrs. Harrington turned to Alistaire and Rowena, who were waiting patiently by the doorway. "Be good," she said to them. "Mind Claudia and Mary Anne. And have fun!"

Mrs. Harrington kissed the children. Before I knew it, Mary Anne, Rowena, Alistaire, and

I were leaving the Dakota. We came to a stop on the sidewalk.

"What do you guys want to do today?" asked Mary Anne. "See tall buildings?"

"Oh, I can see tall buildings right here," Alistaire replied solemnly, looking up. "Rowena and I would very much like to go to Central Park, though."

"We saw pictures of it in Alistaire's book," added Rowena. "We saw a lovely carousel and animals in a zoo — "

"And a man selling toys that were tied to sticks!" interrupted Alistaire.

"Okay. A day in Central Park," agreed Mary Anne cheerfully.

"Is it *very* far away?" asked Rowena.

I put my hands on her shoulders and turned her so that she was facing Central Park West. "Look across the street," I said. "See those trees?"

"Yes," said both Rowena and Alistaire.

"Well, that's the park."

"Oh!" cried the kids. "Brilliant!"

I snuck a peek at Mary Anne. I could tell she was as enchanted by the Harringtons as I was. Rowena and Alistaire spoke with wonderful accents. They were endlessly polite but didn't seem stuck-up. They were eager and curious and delighted by each new sight or activity.

The four of us walked through the park.

"Want to go to the zoo first?" asked Mary Anne.

"Oh, yes!" cried Rowena. "I want to see some bears. But no snakes, thank you."

The walk to the zoo was on the long side, but the kids didn't seem to mind. They ran ahead of us (not too far, though), and once I saw Alistaire jump up, swat at a leafy tree, and cry, "We're *in* Central *Park!*"

We reached the children's petting zoo before we came to the main part of the zoo. "Would you like to pet some animals?" asked Mary Anne.

The kids did, of course, so I forked over forty cents (the petting zoo costs just ten cents per person, and always will), and we walked through a narrow building and out into the sunshine again.

"Oh!" exclaimed Rowena immediately. "A goat!"

Alistaire and Rowena ran from pen to pen and exhibit to exhibit. When they had had their fill, we left to explore the rest of the zoo. On the way, we passed several vendors. Most of them were selling food — ice cream, pretzels, sodas, hot dogs. But Alistaire barely noticed the food (although Rowena looked longingly at the Good Humor stand). Instead he exclaimed, "There's the man selling toys on sticks! It's the man from my book!"

Well, naturally, there are probably thousands of people who sell inflatable toys tied to sticks, but apparently the only one Alistaire had seen until now was between the covers of a book.

"Would you like to buy a toy?" I asked the kids. Then I added generously, thinking of the bills in my purse, "You can each have one."

With great excitement, and after much discussion, Alistaire chose a rocket ship and Rowena chose a coiled snake.

"I thought you didn't like snakes," Mary Anne said to her.

"I don't like real ones. Blown-up ones are all right."

Before we walked on, Alistaire turned to the toy seller and said, "I *loved* your book." (The man looked thoroughly confused.)

We spent more than an hour in the zoo. Despite the lovely weather, it wasn't crowded, which was a miracle. As the kids explored things, I kept seeing the same people over and over again — a young man and his *very* noisy little girl; a couple and their baby, who was riding around in a pouch strapped to the mother; a tall man wearing sunglasses and a rain hat; and a mom with two little boys wearing identical outfits but who didn't look a thing alike. This is one reason I ♥ New York. All the different people.

When Rowena and Alistaire tired of the zoo, we walked out, coming to the big Delacorte clock just as it struck the hour and the animal orchestra (statues) moved around and around while music played. We bought lunch from the vendors and ate on a bench in the park.

By the time three-thirty rolled around, the kids had ridden the carousel, oohed and aahed over the statue of a cougar by the roadside, climbed all over the Alice in Wonderland "playground" (another sculpture), and listened intently to a lively brass band that had set itself up on a grassy lawn.

"What did you think of the park?" Mary Anne asked the kids as we were walking back to the Dakota.

"It's great," said Alistaire.

"Can we move into the zoo?" asked Rowena.

The statue of Alice in Wonderland
Central Park

Claudia

Monday

Today is our first art class and Malony and I are realy exited. I cannot wait to go to FAL of NY. I think students who go there alot call it Falny I wonder if i shoud do that right away or wait awhil. Well I am to exited to wright anymore so I guess Ill stop here. Tomorrow I will have more news.

Claudia

I had more news all right, but it wasn't any good. Falny turned out to be the biggest mistake of my life. I was sure of that by the time we broke for lunch. What had happened? I suppose I might as well give you the gory details of my sad story.

I don't know about Mallory, but I was up at the *crack* of dawn on Monday morning. If roosters lived in New York, they would have been crowing when I first woke up. (At least, I think they would have been. I am not all that familiar with roosters.) Anyway, the first time I looked at my watch, it read 4:06. "Four-oh-six!" I muttered. "I don't believe it." I felt wide awake, but soon I drifted to sleep again. When I awoke the second time, my watch read 5:33. Does anyone actually get up at this hour?

I could not go to sleep. I was jumpy, as if a kangaroo were in my stomach. And all I could think about was McKenzie Clarke. If I closed my eyes, I imagined HIS face. I bet, I thought, that he has kind, twinkly blue eyes and looks a little like Santa Claus, except for the cherry nose. If I opened my eyes, I found myself daydreaming about art class. I would impress Mac with my swift and accurate sketching. He would flip through my drawings and say, "Goodness! Where did you study before?"

"Oh, nowhere really," I would reply.

"Nowhere? But this is the work of a creative genius." Then McKenzie Clark would phone my parents, tell them what a find I am, and ask their permission to allow me to study with him privately. He would become my mentor (I think that's the word I'm looking for), and I, after just a few months of study with Mac, would become —

"Claud?" murmured Stacey's voice from among the pillows on her bed. "You better get up now. You don't want to be late for your first day of classes."

Mal and I entered the doors of Falny feeling pretty nervous, as you might have guessed. But my nervousness faded quickly.

As someone once said, "What . . . a . . . *dump!*"

I whispered that to Mal, and she smiled, but she was too scared to speak.

In all honesty, Falny wasn't a dump; it just wasn't what I had expected, which was a grand, Gothic building with a fancy entryway, or maybe something that looked like the Metropolitan Museum of Art. The entrance to Falny was just a set of glass double doors, with brass letters reading FALNY set above them. However, we were somewhat more impressed by the huge classrooms we found on the third, fourth, and fifth floors. Mac's room was #414. We walked inside slowly, Mal clinging to the back of my shirt, like a kindergartner on her first day of school.

"Cut it out!" I whispered loudly.

Mal's response was, "What's with the boxes?"

The two of us came to our senses and walked into the room like the mature young adults we are.

In a ring around the room were our drawing tables. Piled into the center of the room were about thirty cardboard cartons. They weren't stacked neatly, though. They looked like they'd been thrown in and had landed in a tumbled heap. Some boxes rested crookedly inside others, some sat squarely on the floor, some were perched precariously on top of two or three or four cartons.

I looked at Mal and shrugged. Then we settled ourselves at the tables that seemed to be nearest the front of the room. We wanted to work as close to Mac as possible. Other students drifted in and took seats. Nobody said much.

"Do you think I'm dressed okay?" Mallory whispered.

"You look fine," I replied — just as HE entered the room.

Mal gasped. "That's him!"

"SHHHH!" I nudged her elbow. (I don't think Mac heard us.)

McKenzie Clarke was not at all what I had expected. He was short and slim and didn't look a bit like Santa Claus. He was also younger than I'd thought he'd be. He wore thick glasses and seemed quite serious. When a couple of kids called, "Hi," he just nodded, then organized his things on one of the drawing tables. Now he was halfway across the room from Mal and me. I could barely see him.

At nine-thirty on the nose, even though kids were still arriving, and without greeting the class, McKenzie Clarke began to speak. He said, "Today's lesson is intended to make you aware of dimension and perspective when you draw."

"Does he realize he has new students?" Mal whispered to me.

Before I could answer her, the boy next to me raised his hand. "Mac?" he began. "When we . . ."

I didn't hear whatever he said. Instead, I turned to Mal and, barely remembering to keep my voice down, hissed, "That kid just called him 'Mac' right to his face! I wonder if we should."

Mal grinned. I knew she was thinking how great being "in" with Mac would feel. I knew that because I was thinking the same thing. But a few seconds later, my smile faded. "Mom and Dad don't let me call adults by their first names unless I know them really, really well," I said. "We haven't even spoken to Mac yet. I think we better call him Mr. Clarke, at least for awhile."

Mallory nodded.

Then I snapped to attention as Mr. Clarke began to explain the day's assignment. We were supposed to draw the pile of boxes, paying special attention to the corners and angles and to dimension.

Draw those *boxes?* I thought. *All* the boxes? Oh, my lord, how boring. But if that was what Mr. Clarke wanted, then that was what I would do. And I would do a good job.

When Mr. Clarke finished explaining the assignment, he began to walk around the room, speaking briefly to each student. Soon Mal clutched my arm and squealed (quietly), "He's almost here!" She looked pale.

"Hello," Mr. Clarke greeted us solemnly. "You must be some of my new students. May I have your names, please?"

I managed to reply, "Claudia Kishi," without my voice cracking. Then I added, "And that's Mallory Pike. She's my friend. We're from — "

Mr. Clarke cut me off. "Each morning I will tell you what materials to bring the next day. Today you need only sketching pads, which I see you have brought, and pencils." (He handed each of us two pencils and a gum eraser.) "I will circle the room, checking your work from time to time."

"Okay. Thanks for — "

Mr. Clarke had turned to the girl next to Mallory.

"Well," I said. "Time to begin."

Mal nodded. Then she looked from the boxes to her pad. Slowly she picked up a pencil and began to draw. She erased her first line.

Meanwhile, I started sketching quickly, line after line after line. I have been studying art for so long that dimension and perspective are things I don't think about much. Of course, I'm *aware* of them when I work, but they're not something I concentrate on.

I had finished drawing the entire pile of boxes by the time Mac appeared at my table again. Mal was plodding through the assignment, erasing practically every line she drew. Finally, she rubbed a hole in the paper and had to start over again. She worked in the same, slow manner, and was erasing yet another line when I looked up into Mac's face, smiled, and said proudly, "I'm all finished." (I couldn't wait for the next assignment.)

Mac turned my pad around and examined the drawing. After a few moments, he frowned and said, "You work much too quickly, Miss Kishi. Would you please begin again? You don't notice that anyone else is finished, do you? Look around the room."

I looked. Everyone was working busily. Mr. Clarke stepped over to Mal's table. With shaking hands, I flipped to the next page in my sketchbook.

I felt stung. No one had ever examined my work and not said at least one nice thing about it. Was I really so bad? Had I come to New York just to find out that I'm not talented as an artist after all? That *couldn't* be true.

I'm not good at anything else.

But all morning, Mr. Clarke kept looking at my drawings, pausing, and then telling me to do something differently — to work more slowly, to pay stricter attention to angles, and on and on and on. Then he would look at Mal's drawings, smile gently, and tell her she was doing fine. *Fine?* Those laboriously drawn boxes, her paper full of holes, eraser marks, and misshapen angles? I was *sure* my work was better than Mal's. But Mr. Clarke was the expert.

By the time we broke for lunch, I was ready to cry. Mal was on top of the world. What had gone wrong?

Jessi

Monday

Today I went to the ballet — all by myself. There was a special afternoon performance. I had a wonderful time. In the first place, I felt grown-up. In the second place, the ballet was beautiful. I loved every minute, even though I have seen other productions of this ballet. (It was _Swan Lake_.) In the third place ... I met a cute guy. No kidding. I know this may not be important to the rest of you, but

Jessi

it meant a LOT to me. The boy's name is Quint (isn't that romantic?) and he lives here in New York, not too far from Laine. Best of all, he's a ballet dancer, too: Good enough to get into Juilliard. There's just one problem....

On Monday morning, I found myself left on my own. (Well, almost on my own.) My friends got going pretty early. In fact, by the time I woke up, I could hear voices in the living room. I looked over at Mallory's bed. It was empty. I wasn't the last one up, was I? How embarrassing to be such a lazybones at the home of people I barely knew. Especially considering that my friends think I'm an early riser because I'm always talking about waking up before anyone else in my family and practicing for dance class at the *barre* in our basement. Okay, so today I'd slept in instead. So what? It was nothing to get upset over. I planned to exercise *most* mornings.

Jessi

Well, *I* was the only one making a big deal out of things. When I stepped into the living room later (dressed, of course), everyone just said, "Good morning," and "Hi, Jessi!"

"Hi," I replied.

"Did you sleep well?" asked Laine's father.

"Oh, just fine. Thank you." I found out later that over at Stacey's, poor Dawn had lain awake almost all night, terrified (like the night before) by noises from the street and the thought of the fire escape outside the window. I, on the other hand, hadn't heard a thing. Of course, Laine's apartment does have central air-conditioning (and no outdoor fire escapes), so we'd been sleeping with the windows closed. I felt sort of like I was in a hotel.

My friends were discussing the plans for the day.

"Stacey and I are in charge of Rowena and Alistaire again," said Mary Anne. "We're going to be out most of the day. But if anyone wants to come with us, you're welcome to. We'll be seeing the sights."

"I might go with you," said Laine.

"Claudia and I are going to Falny," spoke up Mal. "I'm so excited!"

"What are you going to do?" I asked Kristy.

"I'm not sure yet," she replied. "Maybe go

over to Stacey's and sit around with Dawn again. I'd really like to get *out* a little, but I feel awful for Dawn. Want to come with me, Jessi?"

I paused. I knew I should be a good sport and go along with Kristy, but that wasn't what I *wanted* to do. I wanted to go to Lincoln Center. I wanted to see a dance company perform.

Before I could decide how to answer, Kristy answered for me. "That's okay, Jessi." She smiled. "Baby-sitting for Dawn isn't my idea of a vacation, either."

I relaxed. "Thanks, Kristy," I said. But about an hour later, I found myself alone in Laine's apartment. Mal had gone off to her art classes, Kristy was on her way over to Stacey's, Stacey had shown up here and she and Mary Anne and Laine were heading for the Harringtons', and both Mr. and Mrs. Cummings had left the apartment for meetings or appointments or something.

How was I going to get to Lincoln Center? I had promised my parents that I wouldn't walk around the city alone. At least not too much. Then I had an idea. Would it work? Only if I moved quickly.

In a flash I found my pocketbook, put on some shoes, ran out of Laine's apartment, remembering to lock the door behind me (the Cummingses had given us our own keys), and dashed to the elevator. I knew what floor the Harringtons were staying on, but I'd forgotten the number of the apartment. It didn't matter. When the elevator doors opened, I found myself facing Mary Anne, Stacey, Laine, Rowena, and Alistaire.

"Jessi!" Mary Anne exclaimed.

"Where you you going?" asked Stacey.

"Well . . . I was hoping to go to Lincoln Center," I began. "But I can't go there alone. I was wondering where *you* are going today."

"To the Children's Museum," replied Mary Anne.

"Is that near Lincoln Center?" I asked.

"No," said Laine.

I must have looked as disappointed as I felt, because Mary Anne immediately said, "You know, the kids might like Lincoln Center. We could go there first and then to the museum. Is that okay with you, Jessi?"

"Sure!"

"Good idea," added Stacey. "I don't know if Rowena and Alistaire will be interested in the theaters, but they can see the fake Statue of Liberty that's nearby. It's fun to look for. And I think they'll like the fountain."

Jessi

So we set off for Lincoln Center.

When we were standing across the street from it, Laine pointed to the complex of buildings and said, "There you go, Jessi."

I gasped.

"What?" shrieked Mary Anne. "A roach? A rat?"

I giggled. "You sound like Dawn. No, it's just that Lincoln Center might be the most beautiful place I've ever seen."

"Look at the fountain!" cried Rowena, pointing.

But I was looking at the Metropolitan Opera House, at the New York State Theater, at Avery Fisher Hall, at the Vivian Beaumont Theater, at the Juilliard School, at Alice Tully Hall. It was hard to believe that those wonderful places — and more — were located in one complex of buildings.

We walked across the street, my mind filled with thoughts of grand performances — plays, ballets, operas, the New York Philharmonic.

"I've just got to see a ballet," I said to Stacey. "And I think there's a special afternoon performance today. I'll stay with you until it begins, and then you guys or Laine could meet me when it's over. . . . Puh-*lease?*"

Lincoln Center -- maybe Jessi will dance there some day!

* * *

So that was how I wound up in a seat in the New York State Theater, watching the New York City Ballet perform *Swan Lake.*

I was in awe. At one point, I even found myself holding my breath. The dancers, their costumes, the wide stage . . . Now I couldn't decide which was more beautiful — Lincoln Center or the scene before my eyes.

When the curtain came down at intermission, I sighed happily.

"Like it?" asked the person sitting next to me.

I'd been so engrossed in the ballet that I hadn't even noticed the boy on my right. He was about my age, with dark, curly hair, wide brown eyes, and skin that was just slightly lighter than mine. And he had the long, lithe body of a dancer.

He was THE most gorgeous guy I had ever seen.

I couldn't believe he was talking to me. Boys never notice me, and I almost never notice boys. What do you *say* to a boy? At least I had an answer to his question. "Like it?" I repeated. "I love it! It's incredible."

The boy nodded. "Every time I see it, I like it better."

Jessi

"See what? This production? Do you live here in New York?"

"Yeah. This is the fifth time I've been here. I mean, to see *Swan Lake.* I'm going broke, but it's worth it."

I took a chance. "Are you a dancer?"

His face reddened. "Um . . ."

"Because I am. I've studied for years. I live in Connecticut, though."

Now he grinned. "My name's Quint."

"I'm Jessi." (Talking to boys is easy, I thought.)

"And I *love* ballet," Quint went on.

"Well, *are* you a dancer?"

"Yes," Quint replied, looking pained. "I take lessons on Saturdays. My teacher says I'm good enough to get into Juilliard."

"Wow!" I was impressed. Juilliard is a famous school of the performing arts, and getting into it isn't easy. "That's fantastic. When are you going to audition?"

Quint looked away. "I'm not," he muttered.

"Oh. Really expensive, huh?"

"No, it's not that. You don't understand. You're a girl."

(What did that have to do with anything?)

"And you're a boy," I said.

"Exactly. The guys in my neighborhood

tease me all the time. When they found out about the dance lessons they began calling me a sissy. Now I have to *sneak* to lessons. Once a week is hard enough. Can you imagine if I went to Juilliard full-time?"

"Yes," I answered firmly. "It would be wonderful. Forget about those guys. If you want to be a dancer, then be a dancer."

Quint smiled. "Thanks," he said, but he was shaking his head. Then he looked at me, frowning. "Well, maybe. Hey, can I have your phone number?"

I blanked out. I couldn't remember Laine's number, but Quint didn't mind. Instead, he wrote down *his* number and address, and handed the slip of paper to me.

I spent the rest of the afternoon as aware of Quint as I was of the ballet.

Would I find the courage to call him?

I wasn't sure at all.

Mallory

Monday

What a wonderful day! Claudia and I took two classes with Mac, one in the morning, one in the afternoon. I'm in love with Mac--- and he really likes my art. He is always complimenting my work. Well, enough bragging. When classes were over, Claud and I went to Stacey's apartment, and soon everyone joined us, even Laine. Then Mr. McGill took us to Chinatown for dinner. It was so, so fun. Now I think I know why Mary Anne ♥'s New York.

Mallory

To be perfectly honest, the day was not as good as I made it sound in the notes I wrote for Claudia. But I didn't think I could say what the problem was. That's because the problem was *Claudia.*

Monday started off okay. When Claud and I had finally found Falny and our classroom, we were nervous about school and meeting Mac. But we were excited, too. We kept pointing at things and giggling.

Then Mac began the morning class.

We were working on perspective and some other thing. In the middle of the classroom was this big jumble of boxes. We were supposed to draw them. It was a tough assignment, and not at all what I'd thought I'd be doing at Falny. I wanted to improve my drawing so that I could illustrate my stories better. I needed to learn to draw bunnies and mice and fat mushrooms and cute little bugs. I needed to learn to draw cats wearing clothes. That kind of thing. But if Mac thought drawing boxes would help, then I would do it. The only problem was that it was *really* hard. I hadn't taken art classes the way Claud had. I wasn't used to assignments like this. I was glad the class lasted for several hours, because

that was how long I needed to sketch those boxes. I worked very slowly. I erased things and started over. I was really embarrassed by how awful my paper looked.

Especially when I glanced over at Claudia's work and noticed two things about it. 1. It was *good*. 2. She could sketch quickly, like those artists on TV. When I saw Mac heading our way, I wanted to cry. But guess what. Mac did not tell Claud her work was good. He told her to start over again and to slow down. Then he said that my work *was* good! At first Claud just looked hurt. But when Mac came back to us and said the same things again, Claud looked like she wanted to kill me. Honest.

Well, I could understand. Claud was supposed to be the artist. But Mac never said anything nice to her. And he said plenty of nice things to me.

"Teacher's pet," Claudia would whisper when Mac was out of earshot.

"I can't help it," I'd reply.

I wished Mac would make at least *one* nice comment to Claud, just to even up things a little.

The afternoon was no better. We had to draw all those darn boxes *again*. They'd been moved around so that they were in a new arrangement. How boring. The worst part, though, was that Claud couldn't seem to do *any*thing right. By the end of the class, she was barely speaking to me.

I tried to be cheerful. "Isn't Falny great?" I said.

"Ha!" was Claud's reply.

We stepped outside to hail a cab to Stacey's apartment. I copied what I thought I had seen Stacey do in this situation. I stood halfway out in the street, waved my arms and yelled, "TAXI!"

Someone grabbed me from behind and pulled me to the sidewalk.

I gasped.

"What's the matter with you, Claud?" I exclaimed. "You scared me to death. I thought you were a mugger."

"You look like a tourist," said Claudia.

"I *am* a tourist."

"But you don't have to let everyone in New York know that."

Claud hailed a cab for us. We rode to Mr. McGill's in silence.

A couple of hours later, we were ready to leave for Chinatown. Stacey's father, Laine, I, and the other members of the BSC were

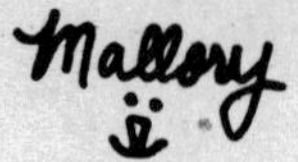

jammed into Mr. McGill's living room, sipping sodas and planning the evening.

"We can take the subway there," said Mr. McGill. "But we'll take cabs back."

"Separate ones, I hope," muttered Claudia.

I stuck my tongue out at her. (She did not see this because she wouldn't look at me. She was pretending I didn't exist.)

"See what I mean?" I whispered to Jessi. "She's been like this ever since the morning. What a jerk."

"Ignore her," said Jessi sympathetically.

"I would, except that she's already ignoring me."

"Okay, let's get a move on," said Mr. McGill.

The steps down to the subway entrance were dirty. They smelled.

"Pee-yew!" I exclaimed.

"Oh, grow up," said Claudia.

"Is this the *only* way to the subway?" asked Dawn, who was standing by herself at the top of the stairs.

"No," replied Stacey, "there are lots of other entrances. But they all look like this. Come *on*, Dawn."

"I think I'll make out a will tonight," Dawn

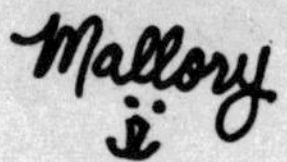

whispered as she rushed by me. "If I live that long."

We managed to reach the token booth, to buy tokens, and to find our platform safely. I felt like a mouse in an underground maze.

"I feel like an ant in an ant farm," said Jessi just then. (Best friends often think alike. At least, Jessi and I do.)

A subway train roared into the station. It stopped, the doors opened, and people poured out. Then my friends (well, my six friends and my one ex-friend) boarded the train and found seats. Dawn positioned herself between Mr. McGill and Kristy (who may be short, but she's fearless). Dawn looked amazed when Stacey's father finally called out, "Okay, girls. The next stop is ours. Get ready for Chinatown!"

"I'm still *alive*," said Dawn in awe.

We climbed another flight of dirty, smelly stairs and found ourselves in a different world.

"Whoa. Are you sure we're still in New York?" I murmured.

"Dweeb," Claud murmured back.

"It does seem like a different world," agreed Mr. McGill.

We really could have been in China. Or I

Mallory

guess we could have, since I haven't been to China. Anyway, this is how I thought it might look.

Around us were low buildings. The signs on some of them were in both English letters and Chinese characters. Others were only in Chinese.

"Hey, look at that phone booth!" cried Jessi.

We all turned to look. It was painted red and shaped like a pagoda.

Mr. McGill led us around a corner, and we found ourselves on a narrow street with narrow sidewalks.

"Cool!" exclaimed Claudia. (She actually sounded excited. She must have forgotten about McKenzie Clarke and the boxes.) "I bet there's good shopping here."

We were standing by a tiny store. Crowded into the window were all sorts of treasures — fans, chopsticks, embroidered shoes, small toys. Nearby stood several racks of T-shirts as well as two racks of postcards.

"Oh, we *have* to go in!" said Mary Anne.

So we did. We bought tons of souvenirs. (I bought a fan for myself and a toy for each of my brothers and sisters.)

When we left the store we walked through the tangle of streets. We passed markets and

Our trip to Chinatown

restaurants, the windows of which were actually aquariums with huge (weird) fish swimming through murky water. We passed people selling fireworks. We passed more of the shops like the one we'd bought souvenirs in. We began to yawn.

"Dinnertime," announced Stacey's father, and he led us into a tiny restaurant with linoleum floors, hard plastic chairs, and tables with no cloths covering them. Almost no one was eating there.

"I don't think these empty tables are a very good sign, do you?" I whispered to Jessi. "Why isn't anyone eating here?"

"Because it's a dive?" she suggested, making a face.

But it wasn't a dive. The food was fantastic and the people who waited on us were really nice. They didn't speak much English and we didn't speak *any* Chinese, but it turned out that the restaurant was run by two sisters and their husbands. Stacey tried to explain to them about the BSC. We ended up laughing, and our waiter gave us extra fortune cookies. My fortunes weren't exactly *fortunes*. They were advice — on how to get ahead in the world and how to get along with people. (I slipped that second fortune onto Claudia's plate.

Mallory

When she noticed it, she read it, glanced at me, and simply muttered, "Teacher's pet.")

We had to hail three cabs in order to get everyone back to Laine's and Stacey's. I was extra glad that Claudia and I were staying at different apartments. However, I would have to face her the next morning.

Kristy

Tuesday

I just could not baby-sit for Dawn again. I felt sorry for her, but I did not come to New York City to sit around in an apartment and watch Dawn clean it. I wanted to see the sights. And I had promised David Michael, Karen, and Andrew that I would "go to Central Park for them." So today Jessi and I explored the park. We saw all sorts of chilly things, but the best part was the surprise we found on the way back to Laine's.

Tuesday morning, Stacey and Mary Anne headed for the Harringtons' again, Claud and Mal went to art school, Laine went shopping with her mother, and Dawn barricaded herself in Mr. McGill's apartment (for the third day in a row).

"Are you going to stay with Dawn again?" Jessi asked me after breakfast.

I shook my head. "I feel guilty, but I just can't. I've spent two days with her. You know what she does over there now?"

"What?"

"She cleans the apartment while Mr. McGill is at his office. Did you notice how neat it was last night?"

"Neater than it was on Saturday," said Jessi.

"Yeah. Mr. McGill had a nice, half-sloppy bachelor pad. Now Dawn is playing housekeeper. I bet Stacey's father can't even find most of his stuff. Dawn keeps organizing things."

"Poor Dawn."

"Poor Mr. McGill!"

"So what are you going to do today?" Jessi wanted to know.

"I'm not sure. How about you?"

Jessi shrugged. "I kind of want to go to Central Park, but — "

"Let's go, then!" I exclaimed. "The weather's beautiful."

So we left for the park. The last time I'd been there I was with Stacey, Mary Anne, Dawn, Claud — and a pack of children we were taking care of. Now I could wander through the park like a regular person. No stopping every five minutes to buy a soda, tie a shoe, or look for a bathroom.

"Ooh," said Jessi as we entered the park. "This is just like last night in Chinatown: I feel as if we've walked into another world."

"I know what you mean. A forest right in the middle of the city."

"It smells so good. What happened to the car exhaust?"

I grinned. "I don't know. But I'm glad it's gone."

"Boy, look at all those dogs," said Jessi.

Everywhere, people were exercising their dogs. A woman in a jogging suit ran by with her rottweiler. An old man walked slowly by with a pair of ancient bassett hounds. A younger man, dressed in jeans and a T-shirt, walked briskly holding a bouquet of leashes. At the other ends of the leashes were *nine* dogs, different breeds and sizes. ("I think he's a professional dog walker," I said to Jessi.) We also saw a couple out walking their tabby cat! The cat looked perfectly happy to be on a leash.

"Oiny," Jessi whispered, giggling.

"What?"

"Oiny. That's something Daddy says. O-I-N-Y. It stands for 'only in New York.' "

I laughed, too.

Jessi and I walked around for nearly two hours. We watched roller skaters weave in and out of tin cans on homemade obstacle courses. We saw people rowing boats on the pond. We saw a *long* line of people and found out they were waiting to get tickets to something called Shakespeare in the Park. They wanted to see the production so badly that they were going to wait *all day*. The show didn't begin until the evening. We saw sunbathers and skateboarders and bike riders.

Finally we grew tired.

"Let's get ice cream," suggested Jessi.

So we did. We found a stand and each bought a double-scoop cone. Then we headed back to Laine's, licking our cones fast to keep the ice cream from dripping.

We had reached a quieter section of the

park, away from most of the activity, when I thought I heard a noise. I stopped in my tracks.

"What is it?" asked Jessi, turning around.

"Shh," was my reply. "Listen."

We listened. And then I heard it again — a pitiful whining.

"It's coming from over there!" I pointed to some shrubs by the path. Then I sprinted toward them. (I dropped my cone.)

"Be careful!" called Jessi.

"I will." Delicately, I parted the bushes. I knew that what I was doing could be dangerous. If a sick animal were hiding there, it could bite me. I should have been wearing gloves. But I wasn't. When I peered into the leafy darkness, the only thing that happened was that the animal whined again.

"It's a dog!" I cried. "It's little, but I don't think it's a puppy."

"Is it hurt?" asked Jessi.

"Come here. Come here, boy," I called softly.

The dog crept forward. In the sunlight, I could see that it was dirty and scruffy, but it didn't seem either sick or hurt. In fact, it spotted my ice cream cone, bounded over to it, and began to lick it happily.

"He looks kind of like Louie," I said to Jessi. "He must be part collie." (Louie was this wonderful collie that was our family pet for years. He died not long after we moved into Watson's house. We miss him a lot.)

"Hey, boy. Where do you belong?" I asked the dog. I looked for his tags, but he wasn't wearing a collar.

"He must be lost. Or abandoned," said Jessi.

"That does it. I'm taking him home."

"To Laine's?" asked Jessi.

"Well, yes. First. But then I'll bring him to Stoneybrook with me."

"Kristy . . ."

"Don't say a word!" I picked up the dog, threw out what was left of the cone, and marched back to the Dakota, Jessi following me. We were across the street from Laine's building when something occurred to me. "I bet the dog won't be allowed in the Dakota," I said. "Lots of apartment buildings don't allow pets."

"What are you going to do?" Jessi wanted to know.

"Sneak him in. You help me. Create a distraction so I can get him by the security guard. Faint or something."

Kristy

"I am *not* going to faint," said Jessi. "I'll ask for directions."

Jessi was great. I have never heard anyone sound more confused. "Lincoln Center is *west* of here?" she repeated. "And south? Which way is west? . . . I'm a tourist."

When the guard turned his back to point out "west," I ran by him, the dog safely in my arms. But, uh-oh. Now how was I going to get him by the Cummingses? I was in luck. Laine was at home, but her parents weren't.

As I ran the dog into the guest bedroom, Laine exclaimed, "You can't keep a dog in here! He's not allowed."

"Tell me about it," I replied.

"We'll have to hide him."

"That's what I was thinking. Let's keep him in the guest bedroom. Your parents wouldn't open the door to the room Jessi and Mal are staying in, would they?"

"I *guess* not," said Laine uncertainly.

"Perfect." I closed the door behind us. Laine and I looked at the dog, who looked eagerly at us. He wagged his tail. I think he *smiled*.

"What are you going to do with him?" Laine asked.

"Take him home. There are so many people

and animals at my house that one more won't matter."

"Are you sure?"

"I'll call Mom at dinnertime. . . . Wait," I said. "I just thought of something. I wonder what Jessi — "

At that moment, Jessi entered the room. She looked very pleased with herself.

"What happened?" I asked.

Jessi grinned. "That poor guard is so mixed up! I asked him for all these directions, then I told him I needed them for tomorrow and I walked inside." (The guards knew who we were. They must have thought Jessi was totally ditsy. Oh, well. She *had* told him she was a tourist.)

"Kristy," Laine spoke up, "that dog is going to have to, um, piddle soon. Don't you think we should put down newspapers for him? And get him some food and dishes and toys and stuff?"

"Definitely." I handed over the rest of my souvenir money to Jessi and Laine, who agreed to go shopping while I dog-sat.

When they returned, we played with our new pet for awhile. Finally, I decided it was time for me to call home.

Kristy

Mom wasn't there, but Watson was. I told him the story of the dog. "So can I keep him?" I asked.

"Absolutely not," replied Watson.

Uh-oh.

Mary Anne

Tuesday

What a day! Being a tourist is tiring. Or maybe caring for two kids is tiring. At any rate, something had completely worn me out by late in the afternoon. We did do an awful lot of walking, though.

Guess what. The weirdest thing happened. Someone is following Stacey and the kids and me. Actually, I think he's just following Alistaire and Rowena. Stacey says I'm crazy. But I see this guy in sunglasses everywhere.

Mary Anne

Stacey and I had planned a heavy schedule of activities for Tuesday. We just kept thinking of things to do. Then, while we were walking around, we found other things to do. That's what I love about New York. Stuff is happening all the time. You never know what you'll discover.

"Okay," said Stacey cheerfully as we ushered Alistaire and Rowena outside the Dakota on Tuesday morning. "We're off to the Museum of Natural History."

"To see the dinosaurs!" added Rowena.

"The dinosaur *skel*etons," Alistaire corrected her. "Just bones, remember?"

"Right. Just bones," repeated Rowena.

"There's also a huge whale I think you'll like," I said.

"A real one?" asked Rowena.

"A *model!*" said Alistaire impatiently. "We're going to a museum, not a zoo."

Rowena made a face at Alistaire. I was glad to see that. Sometimes children who are *too* polite and proper are scary.

Before we reached the museum, though, we were distracted by a street fair.

"Cool! Look at that!" exclaimed Stacey, pointing down a side street.

I saw that two blocks had been roped off. Stalls and stands were set up along both sides of the street. A woman was selling balloons. Kids were walking around with Popsicles and cotton candy. A small Ferris wheel was operating at the end of the second block.

"May we go to the fair? Please?" cried Alistaire.

"Please?" added Rowena.

Stacey and I looked at each other. "Why not?" I said.

"Oh, thank you!" exclaimed the children.

As usual, the Harringtons had given Stacey and me plenty of spending money. The four of us roamed the stalls, examining the "rummage" items for sale. (Rowena wanted to buy a music box, but it cost more than a hundred dollars. "It's a genuine antique," a man assured us, but I knew better than to buy a hundred-dollar toy without the Harringtons' permission.)

"I'm thirsty," Alistaire announced, so we stood on a line to buy lemonade.

Nearby was a man wearing sunglasses and a rain hat. He was looking around the fair. Lots of families had come to the fair, but plenty of people had come alone, too. (I didn't think I would enjoy a fair alone.)

When we had paid for our lemonades (and they were ex*pen*sive, as lemonades go) we walked around some more. Stacey bought balloons for the children. "You can't take them into the museum, though," she warned them.

"That's all right! That's all right!" said Rowena. "We'll tie them to something outside and get them when we're done."

Alistaire and Rowena finished their drinks. They rode the Ferris wheel. (The man in the hat and sunglasses watched them from a distance, smiling. I smiled, too. The kids were shrieking with delight.)

After their ride, we left the fair.

"How do you like my pet dog?" Rowena asked as the four of us walked slowly toward the museum.

"Your what?" I said. I was holding one of her hands. In her other hand was her balloon. It bobbed along beside us.

"My pet dog," Rowena said again. She pointed to the balloon. "See him? He's on his leash. His name is . . . Travis. Travis Balloon."

"*My* balloon is a cat," said Alistaire. "Fat Cat. He likes to walk on his leash."

"Very nice," I pronounced.

"They're not *really* animals," Rowena whispered to me. "Just make-believe."

"Oh," I whispered back. "Thank you."

Near the museum, Stacey and I spotted a bicycle rack. "We'll tie your . . . pets to the rack," said Stacey.

"But I think you should know," I added, "that your pets might be gone by the time we get back here."

"Why?" asked Alistaire.

Why? Because sometimes things are stolen. But how could I explain that to a seven-year-old and a four-year-old? Luckily I didn't have to.

"Because pets run away," Rowena informed her brother.

"Oh. Right."

Whew.

Inside the museum, Stacey, Alistaire, Rowena, and I headed directly for the dinosaurs. Alistaire was awed. "Look at all those skeletons," he said reverently. "How brilliant."

"Bones, bones, bones," sang Rowena. "Is that what we look like inside?"

"*No*, silly!" cried Alistaire, but I wasn't paying much attention to him. I had just turned around and spotted a man in sunglasses and a rain hat ambling around the doorway to the room we had entered.

"What is that? A new style?" I said aloud.

Alistaire's dinosaur bones

"Huh?" replied Stacey.

"Every other man I've seen today is wearing a rain hat and a pair of sunglasses. I wonder why this guy is wearing sunglasses indoors."

Stacey shrugged. "Hey, this is New York. Anything goes."

We poked around the museum until the kids grew bored. Then we rode an elevator to the bottom floor and looked around the gift shop. Alistaire bought a T-shirt with a picture of a stegasaurus on the front. Rowena bought . . . That's funny. I can't remember what she bought. Maybe that's because it was in the gift shop that I first felt that creepy sensation of being watched. I looked all around the shop. The only person staring at me was a baby riding in a pack on his mother's back. When I looked at him, he smiled and drooled. The creepy feeling was not coming from the baby — but it didn't go away.

We ate a quick lunch in the fast-food restaurant near the shop. Then we left the museum. Stacey whispered to me, "Let's go right to the library without passing the bicycle rack. Maybe the kids will forget about their balloons."

At almost the same time, Rowena said, "Let's see if our pets are still here."

Inwardly, I groaned. Stacey and I had no choice but to go back to the bike rack.

From quite a distance, Alistaire let out a yell. "There they are!"

Stacey and I peered ahead. Sure enough, two balloons were blowing back and forth in the light breeze.

"Well, I'm surprised," said Stacey.

"Me, too," I replied. "These balloons are red and blue. They were red and *green* when we left. Rowena wanted a green balloon, remember?"

"I guess," said Stacey slowly.

By then, the kids had untied the balloons and helped each other fasten them to their wrists. Rowena didn't say a thing about the color of her balloon.

Maybe I was losing my mind.

Our next stop was a nearby branch of the public library. Stacey had a New York Public Library card and thought the children might have fun choosing books to read during their stay in the city. Then I discovered that a storytelling hour was to be held in the children's room that afternoon. We had plenty of time to look for books before the program began.

When we reached the library, we stood outside and I wondered what to do about the balloons. This time, Alistaire saved me. "Let's let our pets go, Rowena," he said. "They want their freedom."

So the children released the balloons and watched them float above the branches of a tree and then behind a tall building.

In the library, the kids looked solemnly through the shelves of children's books, and each chose four, which Stacey checked out for them. She waited on line, standing just two places ahead of *another* man wearing sunglasses and a rain hat. I shivered — and realized I'd had that feeling of being watched while Rowena and Alistaire browsed through the books.

The weirdest thing, though, was that the man came to hear the storyteller, even though he was alone.

"You don't think that's strange?" I asked Stacey. "Do you see any other adults without children in this room?"

"No," she replied. "But big deal. So he likes storytelling. It's a lost art, you know."

However, Stacey *did* agree that something was odd when I saw yet another guy wearing sunglasses and a rain hat as we walked back to the Dakota. He was about a block behind us.

"*Wait* a minute!" I cried softly. "Stacey, how stupid I've been! I haven't been seeing strange men all over the city. I've been seeing the *same strange man*. We're being followed."

"Why would anyone follow *us?*" asked Stacey.

"Well, maybe he's not following you and me," I replied. "Maybe he's following Alistaire and Rowena. Their parents are pretty important."

"You're crazy," was Stacey's answer. "And don't you dare say a word about this when we get back to the Harringtons'. Do you want us to lose the job?"

"I'd rather lose the job than the children."

Stacey just shook her head.

Dawn

Tuesday

Oh, please. Somebody get me out of here. I want to go back to Stoneybrook. This morning on the news I heard about two murders. TWO new murders in ONE night. Can you imagine? No one has been murdered in Stoneybrook in all the time I've lived there. But here it seems that people are murdered every day. Well, New York is a little larger than Stoneybrook. Still...

Dawn

Nobody stayed at home with me on Tuesday. I understood that Mr. McGill had to work, and that Claud, Mal, Stacey, and Mary Anne were busy. But what about Kristy and Jessi? They abandoned me. Maybe they didn't realize how frightened I was.

I had made the major mistake of listening to the news in the morning. That was when I heard all that murder stuff. (I was pretty sure I'd never see my friends alive again.) Maybe I should call Mom and tell her I was coming home early. No. I couldn't do that. The rest of the BSC members would never let me forget it. Even Jessi and Mal weren't scared, and they're two years younger than I am. I knew I had to stay.

On Monday, when Kristy had come over, we'd watched several hours of television. In fact, since I'd arrived in New York, I'd watched a considerable amount of TV. I'd watched so much that by Tuesday I thought I'd go crazy if I saw one more toothpaste commercial or even if I saw one more *I Love Lucy* rerun. (The day before, I had discovered that I'd memorized Lucy Ricardo's "Vitameatavegamin" speech: "Hello, friends. Are you tired, rundown, listless? Do you poop out at parties? Are you unpopular? . . .")

So I'd tried listening to the radio. But the music was interrupted every ten minutes by news reports. In desperation, I cleaned out Mr. McGill's refrigerator. Then I organized the food in it. When that was done, I decided I really ought to organize his china, too. I was just putting the last saucer in place when . . . the doorbell rang.

I dove for cover. How had someone gotten upstairs if I hadn't buzzed him in? Maybe it was Stacey. She'd let herself into the building, and now she wanted me to let her in the apartment.

The bell rang again. I crept to the door and squinted through the peephole.

Yikes! A boy was standing in the hallway. And he looked like a real creep. But when he called, "Hello?" I felt I had to answer him.

"Who is it?" I yelled.

"My name is Richie," the boy replied. "Richie Magnesi. I live downstairs. Are you Stacey? Your father said you'd be visiting."

Well, I had heard Mr. McGill mention the Magnesis, but how did I know this boy really *was* Richie Magnesi?

Dawn

I decided not to open the door, so I said loudly, "Stacey's not here. I'm Dawn, a friend of hers. I'm visiting."

"Can I come in? I'm sorry to be so pushy, but I have a broken ankle and I'm supposed to stay off my feet. I can't go out. I'm bored stiff."

I looked through the peephole again. Richie was supported by a pair of crutches.

This could still be a ruse. I hesitated.

Richie spoke again. "I *am* supposed to be *off* my feet," he reminded me. "I'm supposed to keep my foot propped up."

"You're Richie *Magnesi?*" I replied.

"*Yes.*" He sounded impatient. He reached . . . for a gun? . . . Oh. No, just into his pocket. He held a card up to the peephole. "That's my student I.D.," he shouted. "See? I am the one and only Richie Magnesi."

I laughed. Finally, I unlocked the door. I opened it slowly.

Richie hobbled inside and headed for the couch. He sank onto it, then gently lifted his leg onto a footrest. "Ahhh," he said. "Thanks, Dawn."

"You're welcome." I was hovering around, not sure what to do. "Would you like a soda?" I asked, when Richie had settled himself.

"Sure. That would be great."

By that time, I felt a little silly. I poured a soda for Richie and a glass of juice for me. I carried both drinks into the living room.

"So you're a friend of Stacey's?" Richie asked.

I nodded. (I had finally decided it was safe to sit down.) "My name is Dawn Schafer. I live in Stoneybrook. Stacey and I go to the same school."

"Oh. I've never met Stacey. But I visit Mr. McGill sometimes. He knows about my ankle. Anyway, he said his daughter would be visiting for two weeks and that I should introduce myself to her."

"How did you break your ankle?" I couldn't help asking.

Richie looked sheepish. "Skating. It wasn't even my fault. I have these new roller blades and I was in Central Park and this guy ran into me with his bicycle. That was all. When I fell, I broke my ankle. I could *feel* it break. I knew it was broken before I even sat up."

"Ew," I said.

"Yeah. I have to wear this cast for *eight weeks.*"

"How many more to go?"

"Six. I'm not even halfway there. But soon

I'm going to get a walking cast. I won't need the crutches anymore."

"Well, that's good." By then I'd had time to study Richie. His hair was brown and longish. He'd let the back grow into a very chilly little tail. And when he smiled, his cheeks dimpled.

How could I have thought he looked like a creep?

"So how come you're sitting around here without Stacey?" Richie wanted to know. "Are you sick or something?"

I was so embarrassed about the *real* reason I was barricaded in the apartment, that I almost said, "Yes, I am sick." But I didn't want to scare Richie by making him think I was contagious, so instead I replied, "New York makes me a little nervous."

"Another antiurbanist?" said Richie.

"Huh?"

"Never mind. Listen, don't you know what a fantastic place this city is?"

"Two people were *murdered* last night."

"Two out of eight million. That means *your* chances of being . . . um . . . hurt are one in four *million*."

"Oh."

"Have you been to New York before?"

"Yeah. A couple of times."

"Did you really *see* the city? Did you walk through the museums — the smaller ones, like the Frick Collection or the Pierpont Morgan Library? Have you seen Gracie Mansion or taken a walking tour of Greenwich Village? Have you been to the Vietnam Veterans Memorial? Have you walked through Chelsea or the Village, or tasted cannoli or sushi or a cheese blintz?"

"I've had a bagel," I said. "Does that count?"

"Dawn, Dawn, Dawn."

"Richie, Richie, Richie."

We laughed. Then Richie went on, "New York is a *great* place. Except that so many people don't know it. Either they're afraid, so they don't come into the city. Or they're *not* afraid, and they come into the city, but all they do is go from one Gap to another. And maybe stroll through Central Park. But that is *not* discovering the city. I've lived here all my life — "

"Have you ever been mugged?" I interrupted him.

"No! And I go out exploring every chance I get. That is, when my ankle's in one piece. Did you know there's a whole museum about firefighting? Do you know all the famous people who've lived in New York — from Greenwich Village to Harlem?"

Richie was more familiar with the city than anyone I'd ever met, including Mary Anne. He made it sound so exciting that I even considered leaving the apartment. Well, maybe the next day . . .

Claudia

Wensesday

Today our art calss took a feild trip to a place called Rockefeller Center. (I know I spelled that wright because I looked it up.) We drew bildings and scluptuaes there. There are lots of neat things to draw like intresting bildings and a sunken plaza where you can go ice skatting in the winter, and a display of flowers and some murals. I would of had a lot more fun if Mr. Clark liked me but he doesnt he likes Mal though.

Claudia

I don't know why I thought I would like Wednesday's art classes any better than I had liked Monday's or Tuesday's. But I kept hoping. I thought that if I worked *really, really* hard, I would finally do something to please Mr. Clarke. Mallory certainly pleased him — with her sloppy, childlike drawings — but so far, he had not said a single nice thing about my work. I was beginning to wonder if Mr. Clarke was such a great teacher. Maybe he couldn't recognize good work. Or maybe he could — and, after all this time, I was a flop.

We had spent two entire days (four classes) drawing those boxes. I don't ever want to see another pile of cartons. I am not kidding. Even if it means never moving out of my room at home. You can imagine how thankful I felt when, on Wednesday, we took our trip to Rockefeller Center.

Mal and I arrived at Falny slightly early on Wednesday. We didn't want to miss anything. And we wanted to look like dedicated art students in case Mr. Clarke arrived before his class did.

He didn't.

Mal and I sat alone in the room until the other students showed up. Then Mr. Clarke entered. "Are you ready to brave the subway?" he asked with a grin.

"Oh, goody. The subway," I said to Mal. "I just love the subway. Honestly."

"I know you do." Mal smiled.

". . . attention to perspective, dimension, and line," Mr. Clarke was saying.

I realized I wasn't listening to him, which probably was not a good move.

I resolved to pay attention.

Twenty minutes later, Mr. Clarke and our class were squeezing into a subway car. The car was crowded to begin with. Eighteen extra bodies only made things worse. But I didn't mind. Then I thought of something.

"Imagine if Dawn were h — " I started to say to Mal.

Mal didn't hear me. She was busy talking. To McKenzie Clarke.

Mr. Clarke had squeezed himself between Mallory and another student. Now he and Mal were discussing horses. Mr. Clarke liked to sketch them and Mal liked to read about them. But she had trouble drawing them.

"It's their hind legs," said Mr. Clarke. "The hind legs are difficult."

"So are their heads. Hey, has your daughter read *Mustang, Wild Spirit of the West*?"

His daughter? How did Mal know Mr. Clarke had a daughter? Well . . . the two of them *had* spent a lot of time talking. Mostly about books.

I turned away from them. I gazed at the ads in our car. Most of them were for roach spray or little roach hotels.

At last, we pulled into a station and Mr. Clarke announced, "This is it, people. Everyone off. Follow me!"

I made sure I was standing right behind him. But by the time we had shoved our way into the station, about five people were between Mr. Clarke and me. *Darn*. I had even lost Mal, but I didn't want her company just then anyway. So I straggled along behind my class.

However, I felt a little different when we reached Rockefeller Center. It was absolutely gorgeous. Tall office buildings rose to the sky. Mr. Clarke pointed out two beautiful statues. He showed Mal and me the outdoor restaurant, which is an ice-skating rink during the winter. He showed us Radio City Music Hall.

And then he said that the NBC television studios were located in one of the buildings. In those studios are filmed game shows, *Sat-*

urday Night Live, Late Night with David Letterman, the *Today* show, and many others.

Oh, I was dying. I was positive I would see a star. Maybe several stars.

". . . anything that might interest you. Okay, Miss Kishi?"

Yikes. Mr. Clarke had been talking again and I hadn't been paying attention (again).

"Um. Yes — " I glanced at Mallory. She nodded. "Yes. That's fine," I finished up.

Mr. Clarke looked away from me. "We'll stay in this area for about half an hour. Then we'll move on."

The students began to scatter. I looked around and realized we were standing near the restaurant/skating rink. I leaned over a rail and peered at the people eating below me. But I found myself imagining skaters there instead. The tables and chairs and plates of food disappeared. In their place I could see a sheet of silvery ice. Children bundled up in snowsuits worked their way awkwardly around the rink. Older kids flew by them, their jackets open. Adults skated along leisurely, arm in arm.

"Claud?" asked Mal.

"Yeah?" I turned and found her at my elbow, sketch pad and pencil in hand.

"What are you going to draw? Do you know yet?"

"Um . . . no." (I knew perfectly well what I was going to draw, but I planned to surprise Mr. Clarke. I didn't want anyone to copy me.)

"Well, I'm going to draw the outdoor restaurant. From up here. I think that's called a bird's-eye view. Anyway, it makes the angles and dimensions really different."

I watched Mal begin to work. Her angles and dimensions certainly *were* different. I stepped away from her, and began my own drawing of what was below me. I called it "Winter Fantasy." It was a picture of the way I envisioned the ice-skating rink in wintertime.

"Miss Kishi?"

Mr. Clarke was behind me! I turned slowly until I was facing him.

"*What* is *that?*" he asked, pointing to my drawing.

"The skating rink," I replied.

Mr. Clarke waved his hand around, indicating Rockefeller Plaza. "I don't see a skating rink here," he replied.

"But you said there's one in the winter. This is how I imagine it."

"That's very creative, Miss Kishi. But the

assignment is to draw what you see."

As soon as Mr. Clarke moved on to the next student, I tore the sheet of paper off the pad, crumpled it up, and hurled it into a nearby trash can. Before I started a new sketch, I glanced at Mal's drawing. More of the same. Her perspective was *way* off. But had Mr. Clarke said anything to her? No.

I began a new drawing. Ten minutes later, Mr. Clarke checked on me again. I had completed a quick sketch of the restaurant. The *whole* thing.

Mr. Clarke sighed. "You're working too quickly again," he said.

When he turned away, I stuck my tongue out at him.

All right. He wanted me to work slowly? Then I would work slowly.

I worked so slowly that my eyes began to wander. And they landed on . . . Donna Brinkman, the star of *Which Way's Up?*, one of my favorite TV shows. I couldn't believe it. Donna Brinkman . . . It *was* Donna Brinkman, wasn't it? Did Donna Brinkman have two small children? Because this person was waiting impatiently for two little boys to catch —

"Okay, class. It's time to move on," Mac spoke up. "It'll be a bit crowded, but I'd like

Rockefeller Center in the summer

for you to move to Fifth Avenue, where you'll have a view of . . ."

It was time to move? But I hadn't finished anything. I mean, I hadn't finished anything that pleased Mr. Clarke. Well, it was his fault for telling me to slow down. If I hadn't slowed down, I wouldn't have started daydreaming.

"Claud, I didn't finish," Mallory wailed then. "I worked so — "

"Well, I didn't finish, either," I snapped.

Mal looked hurt. Then she stopped talking.

On the way to Fifth Avenue, I thought we passed Elvis Presley, but I don't think so. I mean, I know he's dead, but an awful lot of people *have* spotted him recently. I considered asking Mal if she knew whether Elvis would ever have worn a checked shirt with plaid pants, but I decided not to. I didn't feel like speaking to her for awhile.

Then, ignoring the throngs of people pushing past me, I began an intricate sketch of this long garden that led like a path to the skating rink and restaurant below. Across a small side street rose 30 Rockefeller Center, home of NBC television. I tried very hard not to think about that. I concentrated on the plants, the flagpoles, the lines and corners of the building. Soon I was so caught up in my work that I forgot about TV stars. I forgot about Mallory and Elvis and whether I had any real talent. I even forgot about Mr. Clarke until I became aware that he was looking over my shoulder.

For almost a minute he watched as I sketched (slowly).

Then he walked away without a word. At least he could have said, "Interesting." Or even *smiled*. I would have been grateful for a smile.

At lunchtime, Mal said to me, "I guess you wouldn't want to go to a bookstore, would you. I heard about a huge one nearby. It has — "

"You're right. I don't want to go to a bookstore."

Mal turned away. "Okay."

She went to the bookstore with Mr. Clarke instead.

I sat by myself and ate a pretzel, which was very salty. Apart from that, it had no flavor. I did not care.

Jessi

Thursday

I met Quint on Monday. Today, three days later, I woke up and realized that I hadn't called him yet. Actually, I had thought the same thing on Tuesday and Wednesday mornings, but I'd just been too chicken to pick up the phone. It is not easy to call a boy, especially when you haven't called one before. How come no one ever told me it would be so hard?

Jessi

On Thursday morning I lay in my bed in Laine's guest room (with Kristy's dog beside me) and thought, I should have called Quint on Tuesday. By now he's probably forgotten who I am. I *can't* call him now. If I did and he came to the phone and I said, "Hi, it's me, Jessi Ramsey," and he said, "Who's Jessi Ramsey?" I would *die*. I know I would.

But by late that morning I had decided to risk death. I was alone in Laine's apartment (except for the dog, and for Laine, who was cleaning out her closet), and I was getting bored. Plus, I would be pretty rude if I *didn't* call Quint.

So, very quietly, I picked up the phone in the kitchen. My heart was pounding. My hands grew sweaty. What was I doing? I must be loony, I thought.

I dialed Quint's number. The phone rang three times. Then someone picked it up.

Oh, no . . .

"Hello?"

"Hello — hello, is Quint there?" I asked. My voice shook.

"Just a moment, please." A hand was cupped over the receiver. I heard the voice call, "Quint? Phone for you."

A few seconds later, Quint was on the line. "Hello?" he said. And then, because I suddenly seemed unable to speak, he tried again. "Hello? . . . *Hello?*"

"Quint, it's me," I blurted out. "I mean, hi, this is Jessi Ramsey."

"Jessi! I was hoping you'd call." Quint sounded genuinely glad.

"You were?"

"Sure. Why else would I have given you my number?"

Oh, yeah. I tried to laugh. "Well, I'm sorry I took so long. I — I, um — "

Quint interrupted me. "Hey, Jessi, if you're not doing anything today, do you want to come over? We can watch old movies. That is, if you can stand my brother and sister. They're sort of pains."

"No problem," I replied. "I would love to watch old movies, and I'm good with kids. I baby-sit all the time."

"Great. We'll have a Fred Astaire and Ginger Rogers festival."

"I'll be right there."

When we got off the phone, I looked at the paper on which I'd written Quint's address. I didn't think Quint lived too far away. Still, I wasn't allowed to walk around the city by myself.

Jessi

"Laine?" I said. I stood in the doorway to her room.

"Yeah?" Laine's reply was muffled. It came from deep within her closet. On the floor around the closet were mounds of clothes, papers, books, stuffed animals, boxes, and crumpled shopping bags. Her parents had told her to clean out her closet before it exploded.

"I need some help."

Laine emerged from her closet, looking dusty and rumpled. "What's wrong?"

I explained to her about Quint.

Suddenly Laine began to sound like my parents. "Gosh, I don't know," she said. "You're going over to this guy's apartment, and you've only met him once?"

"Well . . . yes. But he's *really* nice. And it's not like we'll be there alone. His mother and brother and sister will be there, too."

In the end, Laine agreed to walk me to Quint's, but only if she could come upstairs and meet Quint's family. She made certain to write his name, address, and phone number on a piece of paper.

"Why?" I asked.

"It's just safer, Jessi. Trust me. Someone should always know where you are."

"Because I'm eleven?"

"No!" Laine looked exasperated. "It doesn't have anything to do with your age. If I visit a new friend, my mom or dad does exactly what I'm doing now."

"Okay." I wanted to feel grown-up, but I felt like a little kid. Still, I could understand why Laine was being cautious. It was the responsible thing to do.

Laine and I stood outside the door to Quint's apartment. The nameplate under the peephole read Walter. Quint Walter. I liked that name.

I pressed the bell and immediately the door was flung open.

"Hi, I'm Morgan," said a little girl. "Are you Quint's new girlfriend?"

His *new* girlfriend? How many girlfriends did Quint have? I managed a smile, though. "I'm Jessi," I said. "And this is my friend Laine. She's leaving."

"I'm leaving after I meet your mother, Morgan. Is she home?" asked Laine.

Five minutes later, Laine was gone. I could tell that she liked Quint and his family. But that didn't prevent her from calling over her shoulder as she waited for the elevator, "I'll be back at five to walk you home!"

Goody, I thought. "Okay," I said.

Jessi

The elevator arrived, and Laine disappeared behind the door.

I turned to face the Walters. There was Quint's mom, who reminded me a little of my own mother, except that she was very soft-spoken, almost shy. There was Morgan, an imp who liked to play tricks. She was six. And there was Tyler, nine years old. "He's usually lost to the world of computers," Quint told me. "I wish he were today. But he and Morgan are being pills." Mr. Walter was at work. "He's a chemical engineer," said Quint.

"Are we going to have a movie festival, Quint?" asked Morgan. "Are we? Is your girlfriend staying?"

Quint looked pained. "Mom," he complained.

"Mom," said Tyler, imitating his brother.

"Kids," said Mrs. Walter.

"I like his girlfriend," announced Morgan. "Hey, Jessi. Want some ABC gum — ?"

"No, she doesn't want any Already Been Chewed gum," Quint answered for me.

"Morgan, are you and your brother going to be pests today?" asked Mrs. Walter. Tyler answered for Morgan. "No, we're going to be pests tomorrow. Today we plan to be pains. Is that okay?"

"Absolutely not," said Mrs. Walter firmly.

In the end, Tyler and Morgan were banned from the TV room. Quint and I got to watch the videos by ourselves. Quint had rented *Top Hat* and another old movie starring Fred Astaire and Ginger Rogers. We were mesmerized by the dancing, though most of it was tap. Very little was ballet.

"Okay. Who do you like better?" Quint asked as he rewound the second tape. "Ginger Rogers or Eleanor Powell?" (Eleanor Powell was another of Fred Astaire's dance partners.)

"Eleanor, I guess," I replied. "Ginger Rogers usually danced in those long dresses or skirts, so you couldn't see what she was doing. If you wanted to see tapping, you had to watch Fred. But Eleanor didn't hide her legs."

"I like Eleanor better, too," said Quint. "But as far as I'm concerned, nobody beats Fred."

"Male chauvinist!" I exclaimed. "What about Ann Miller?"

Quint grinned. "You win. Want to take a walk? We can return the videos."

"Sure," I replied.

Quint told his mother where we were going. Then we tiptoed out of the apartment before Tyler and Morgan could figure out what we were up to.

Jessi

"Ah, freedom," said Quint, breathing in deeply, as we left his building.

We started down the sidewalk, past a row of old brownstones. Kids were sitting around on the stoops. "What a nice New York scene," I started to say.

But I was cut off. "Whoo! There he goes! The sissy!" cried a boy.

"Yeah! Look. Up in the sky. It's a bird. It's a plane. No, it's . . . sissy-boy!"

"Hey, where are your tights? Where are your pink slippers?"

All around us, kids were taunting Quint.

"Say something," I muttered, elbowing him.

"Shut up!" Quint shouted.

"He can speak," retorted a tall, skinny boy. "Hey, look! Sissy-boy has a girlfriend. She's probably — "

"Leave her alone!" yelled Quint. He dove for the boy.

"Quint, stop!" I cried. I caught him by the back of his shirt.

"Yeah, Quint. Stop! Stop it!" mimicked the boy.

"Come on." I tugged at Quint. We walked to the end of the block and turned the corner.

Jessi

The taunting stopped. We had left the kids behind.

"See?" Quint exclaimed angrily. "See why I can't go to Juilliard, Jessi? Going to Saturday dance classes is bad enough. I try to sneak my stuff by those kids in a bowling-ball bag. But they know there's no bowling ball inside."

I sighed. "The kids *are* cruel, Quint. They really are. But sometimes you have to put up with people like them. I mean, are you going to let a bunch of jerks like them keep you from becoming a dancer? *I* wouldn't let them. Think of them as sore muscles. Something you have to endure. But don't let them stand in your way."

"Those are nice thoughts, Jessi," Quint replied. "But you don't know what it's like. You don't have to walk down my street every day."

Okay. So maybe I didn't know what it was like. But I knew how it felt to dance.

Stacey

Friday

Our two-week vacation is half over. What a drag. I suppose I could look at the situation from another angle and say that we still have a whole week of vacation left. (I could, but I'm not going to. Deep down, I know the truth: our vacation is half over.)

My father did something amazing today. HE TOOK THE AFTERNOON OFF FROM WORK. Now he'll probably work every weekend for the next decade, but — we had a terrific afternoon. Dad surprised my friends and me by taking us (plus Laine, Rowena, and Alistaire) on a Circle Line tour around the island of Manhattan.

Stacey

The island of Manhattan. That sounds so odd. When I think of islands, I imagine desert islands, with palm trees and coconuts and bananas. But Manhattan *is* an island, long and skinny and surrounded by the Hudson River, the East River, the Harlem River, and New York Bay. And climbing aboard a boat and traveling around Manhattan is a terrific way to see the city and other sights. It's fun, too.

Once I got over the shock of my father's announcement ("I think I'll take the afternoon off"), I started organizing our trip.

"You mean," I said to Dad, "that you're going to take *all* of my friends and me on the Circle Line today?"

"Yup. I can't think of a better way to see Manhattan."

"Can Laine come, too?"

"Sure. Oh, what about Claudia and Mallory? Do they — "

"They're free on Friday afternoons."

"Perfect."

"Wait a sec. What am I thinking? Mary Anne and I are supposed to baby-sit today. We can't abandon Alistaire and Rowena."

"Bring them along."

So we did. While Dad was at his office in

the morning, Mary Anne and I went to the Harringtons'. We asked permission to take the children on the sightseeing tour. Mr. and Mrs. Harrington thought that was a terrific idea. So did the kids.

"Oh, brilliant!" cried Alistaire. "A boat tour!"

"Brilliant!" echoed Rowena.

After lunch, Mary Anne and I helped the kids to dress in the outfits their parents had requested they wear on the boat: Alistaire in gray pants, red suspenders, a red bow tie, and a white shirt; Rowena in a gray skirt, red suspenders, a red headband, and a white blouse.

"I hope they don't get seasick," Mary Anne whispered to me, looking at the newly cleaned and pressed outfits.

"Don't even think about that," I replied.

"What *can* I think about? You told me not to think about the kidnapper, either." (Mary Anne had decided that the man in the sunglasses and rain hat was on a mission to kidnap Alistaire and Rowena and create an international incident which, among other things, would destroy the reputation of the BSC. That, I had said, was ridiculous. We didn't know he was after Alistaire and Rowena. We didn't even know if there *was* just one man, and since Mary Anne's scare at the library, we'd only seen men in rain hats and sunglasses four more times. They were all wearing different jackets.)

"You can think about three hours of nothing but New York sights," I replied. "You'll have a jam-packed afternoon: the Statue of Libberty, the Brooklyn Bridge, Gracie Mansion, where — "

"I know! Where the mayor lives!" Mary Anne was excited. She'd forgotten about seasickness and kidnappers.

At one o'clock that afternoon, Mary Anne, the Harrington children, and I met Dad and my friends at the pier on the Hudson River at 42nd Street. Everyone except Alistaire and Rowena was wearing jeans.

"Well, you guys, get ready for thirty-five miles of sightseeing," said Mary Anne.

"She read the Circle Line pamphlet," Kristy whispered to me. "I think she knows it by heart. Listen to her."

"The scenery comes to *you*," quoted Mary Anne. "Plus prize photo opportunities. Spacious decks. Informative commentators."

I rolled my eyes.

"Come on, everybody," said Dad. "The tour starts at one-thirty."

"Ooh, there's our boat," Alistaire said softly, a few moments later. "It says 'America's Favorite Boat Ride.' Brilliant! And we get to go on it."

We paid our entrance fee and boarded the boat. Alistaire and Rowena walked slowly around the deck, trying to figure out the best place from which to sightsee.

"Over here," Rowena would say.

"No, here I think," Alistaire would reply.

Then they discovered that food was available — snacks and sandwiches and sodas. They'd just eaten lunch, but that didn't seem to matter. I guess buying food almost anywhere is more interesting than eating what comes out of your own refrigerator.

"Let's get them something," I said to Mary Anne. "This *is* a special treat."

"What if they get seasick?"

"All right. No snacks. How about sodas?"

Mary Anne agreed to that, so we bought sodas and then found an empty area by the deck railing, and stood there with Dad and my friends.

A few minutes later we were breezing down the Hudson River.

"Now, everyone," said Mary Anne, "ahead of us you see the Jacob Javits Convention Center. It takes up twenty-two acres, five blocks — "

"Mary *Anne!* We have a *tour guide,*" I hissed. "And I can't hear him."

Mary Anne closed her mouth.

I listened to the guide. So did Dad and Laine. I don't know why, since we were the three native New Yorkers in our group, and no one else was paying attention.

Mary Anne was giving herself her own tour. "The World Trade Center," I heard her murmur. "Two towers, one hundred and ten stories each . . ."

Kristy was whispering to Claudia, "I can't believe we're leaving him completely alone this afternoon." (She meant the dog, which she'd named Sonny.) "Mrs. Cummings is bound to find him. We've just been lucky so far."

Claudia was listening to Kristy — but giving the evil eyeball to Mallory.

Mallory and Jessi were looking in the opposite direction from everyone else, and Jessi was pointing and saying, "There's New *Jer*sey, Mal. My home state. Hello, Oakley!"

Dawn, sandwiched between Kristy and Mary Anne, was staring dreamily into space.

Rowena and Alistaire were alternately concentrating on their sodas and hoping to be sprayed in their faces as the boat chugged through the choppy water.

The man in the hat was reading a newspaper.

Wait a second! I froze. The man in the hat? What was he doing here? Was it the *same* man in the hat? The breeze whipped his newspaper, and as he struggled to hold onto the fluttering pages, I saw the sunglasses. It *was* the same man!

"Mary Anne!" I hissed. I pulled her away from the others. "Don't panic. And keep quiet, okay? Now, *don't panic* — but there's the guy with the hat and glasses."

Mary Anne turned pale. I wondered if her heart was pounding as fast as mine was. We were passing the Statue of Liberty, and everyone was gazing at it. Even the man.

"He's after the children!" Mary Anne whispered. "I know he wants to kidnap them. Remember when we learned about the Lindbergh kidnapping? Remember that guy who took Anne and Charles Lindbergh's baby? A long time ago? Well, after that, a lot of famous people became afraid their children would be kidnapped, too. You know, for ransom money. And they tried to protect their kids by changing their last names and stuff. I just know this guy is after Alistaire and Rowena. Think how important their parents are."

"And think of the ransom the Harringtons could afford to pay," I added.

"Oh, what are we going to *do*? Disguise the children?"

"Dis*guise* them? How? With mustaches and wigs? Come on, Mary Anne."

"Well, do you have a better idea?"

"No. But we are not going to disguise Rowena and Alistaire. We'll just have to watch them every second. Never let them out of our sight. We should probably be holding them in our laps right now," I added.

"Shouldn't we tell the Harringtons about this man?"

"Tell them what? That we're being followed by a bad dresser and that they should alert the fashion police? The man hasn't done a thing. He barely even looks at the kids. We just see him everywhere. That's all."

"I guess you're right," said Mary Anne nervously. "Okay. Never let the kids out of our arms. That's our motto."

"I think 'Never let the kids out of our *sight*' will work just fine."

Nevertheless, Mary Anne grabbed Rowena's hand and I grabbed Alistaire's. We held onto the children as we passed South Street Seaport, sailed under the Brooklyn Bridge and the Triboro Bridge, and gawked at Yankee Stadium. We held onto them as we plowed through the water under the George Washington Bridge.

"The George Washington Bridge?" said Claud. "I thought it was called the Abraham Lincoln Bridge. Isn't — "

"You're thinking of the Lincoln Tunnel," I told her, eyeing the man.

The man had put his paper away. He seemed to be listening to our guide, who was soon directing our attention to Riverside Drive.

The tour was almost over. (In my opinion, it couldn't be over fast enough.)

Mary Anne and I would have to stay on our toes for the next week.

The famous Brooklyn Bridge

Kristy

Saturday

Oh, I am so embarrassed. The worst thing in the world happened yesterday. It happened while my friends and I were on the Circle Line Tour. MRS. CUMMINGS FOUND SONNY. Honest. When Laine and mary Anne and Jessi and Mal and I returned to Laine's apartment after the cruise, we found Mrs. Cummings in the living room. She was sitting on the couch next to... Sonny. I almost died.

Kristy

I bet you think hiding a dog isn't easy.

Well, you're right.

We got away with it for three days, which may have been a miracle, although a few things were working in our favor: 1. Mr. and Mrs. Cummings are very busy and not home a lot. 2. We were able to keep Sonny in the guest bedroom behind closed doors by allowing Laine's parents to think that Mallory has some sort of privacy complex. 3. Sonny was an incredibly well-behaved and well-trained dog.

On Tuesday, when we first found Sonny and spirited him into the apartment, I stayed with him while Laine and Jessi bought dog supplies at the pet store and supermarket. During that time, Sonny got his name. I was lying on Jessi's bed, looking down at Sonny, who was sniffing around the room, and I whispered, "You look *so* much like Louie. It's really amazing. I think I'll call you Son of Louie." But Son of Louie was much too long a name, so I shortened it to Sonny.

That night, my friends and I closed ourselves in the bedroom with Sonny. We had told Mr. Cummings (Mrs. Cummings was out) that we were holding a secret BSC meeting.

This seemed possible, since Stacey, Claud, and even Dawn were visiting Laine that evening. Mr. Cummings smiled and said he would leave us to our own devices (whatever they are). Then I guess we really did hold a sort of BSC meeting, except that Laine isn't a member of the club. For more than an hour we fussed over Sonny. We tossed his new toys to him. We fed him dog treats. And we talked about what we were going to do with him. Since I thought I could soften up Watson by the time we left New York, I wasn't worried about finding a home for Sonny. I was just concerned about hiding him until I could bring him back to Stoneybrook with me, where he would live like a king in our house.

"How are you going to take him out for walks?" asked Jessi. "I can only ask so many stupid questions to distract the guard."

"You probably just need to get him out of the apartment about three times a day, don't you?" said Laine. "Mom and Dad are out pretty often. That'll make things easier."

"I guess," said Jessi.

"And we've got a food supply, and papers on the floor in *case* of an accident. All we have to do is keep Sonny quiet — and he's already quiet — keep him hidden, and keep his food dishes clean. You know, so they don't smell."

"Uh-oh," said Stacey. "Laine, what about Sallie?"

"Who's Sallie?" asked Dawn.

"She comes in to clean our apartment," replied Laine. "Boy, you guys are *really* in luck. Sallie's on vacation for a few weeks and Mom and Dad never bother to replace her while she's away. They just let the dust build up."

"So if we keep the door to our room shut, no one will come in?" asked Mal.

"Nope," said Laine.

And that was how we hid Sonny until Friday afternoon.

I was nervous about Friday. It was the first time I would have to leave Sonny alone for so long with Mrs. Cummings at home. I had made sure to walk Sonny before we left. I fed him and played with him. I put his food, his water, and his toys in plain sight. Then I closed the door to the guest bedroom. With any luck, when we returned from the tour, I would find things as I had left them.

But my luck had run out. As I said before, we walked into the apartment, and there were Mrs. Cummings and Sonny.

"Well, see you later," I said. I turned around to head out the door.

"Oh, no," exclaimed Laine. She grabbed the back of my shirt. "He's your dog, Kristy. Start talking."

"He's Kristy's dog?" repeated Mrs. Cummings. "Then what was he doing in the guest bedroom? That's where I found him, crying away."

"He was crying?" I said.

"Yes. He had to go to the bathroom rather badly."

"Oh. I guess an entire afternoon was too much for him. Poor Sonny." I scratched him behind his ears. "Wait!" I cried suddenly. "Mrs. Cummings, he didn't, um, mess up the carpet, did he?"

Laine's mother shook her head. "No. I got him outside in time."

"What kind of diversion did *you* create?" Jessi asked Mrs. Cummings, with interest.

Mrs. Cummings looked confused.

"She means, how did you get him by the guards?" I said helpfully.

Now Laine looked confused, too. She glanced at her mother.

"Why, I simply walked him outside. As I passed Eddie, he said, 'Nice dog, Mrs. Cummings. I didn't know you had a pet.' And I said, 'Neither did I,' and we both laughed. Then I told him where I'd found the dog and that I'd let him hear the rest of the story as soon as I knew it myself."

I clapped my hand to my forehead. "I am *so* sorry," I cried. "Did you get kicked out of the building? What are you going to do?"

"Kicked out?" said Laine. "Why would we get kicked out?"

"For having a pet. I know they're not allowed in your building."

"Yes they are," said Laine.

"But you said we had to hide Sonny." Now *I* felt confused.

"From *Mom* and *Dad,*" Laine explained. "They've always said I couldn't have a pet. They said pets make too much dirt. You know, shedding their fur and stuff. And I thought, especially with Sallie on vacation — "

I couldn't help it. I burst out laughing. "You mean I've been sneaking Sonny in and out for nothing?"

"I thought you were sneaking around so Mom and Dad wouldn't find out about him." Laine was laughing, too. So was everyone else.

Except Mrs. Cummings.

Laine's mom looked at me thoughtfully and said, "Kristy, what do you plan to do with Sonny? We can't keep him."

I explained that I was busy softening up Watson.

But Mrs. Cummings looked doubtful. "Your stepfather said no, honey?"

"Yeah." I looked at the floor.

"What makes you think he's going to change his mind?"

I shrugged. "Because I want Sonny? Because he reminds me of Louie?"

Mrs. Cummings gave me a Parent Look. "If I were you, I'd start finding Sonny's owner. He might have one, you know. Or start finding him a new owner. Sonny is welcome to stay here until you leave next week. But . . ."

Her voice trailed off. I knew what she had meant to say, though. After that, who knew what would happen to Sonny? The Cummingses wouldn't keep him. What would they do? Drop him off at the dog pound?

I tried to think positively. It was Friday afternoon. I would be in New York until the following Saturday morning. That meant I had about seven and a half days to find either Sonny's former owner or a new owner.

That was possible, wasn't it?

* * *

I went to bed that night feeling pretty subdued. But when I awoke on Saturday, I was full of ideas.

"First thing," I said to Mary Anne and Laine as we lay in our beds, "is to take Sonny to a vet and make sure he's healthy. I'll have a much easier time finding a home for him if he has a certificate of health from a veterinarian."

"Good idea," said Laine.

"I know," I replied. "Except for one thing. I'm broke. I've spent all my money on supplies for Sonny. . . . Hey, that sounds like a Country and Western song! . . . Anyway, I don't have a penny. And vets are expensive."

"There's a good clinic not far from here," Laine informed me. "The doctor's fee is whatever you can afford to pay."

"What if you can afford zero," I asked.

"I'll lend you five dollars," said Laine.

"Me, too," spoke up Mary Anne. "A ten-dollar fee isn't bad."

"Wow, thanks! This is great. I promise I'll pay back both of you — after I'm home and I've earned ten bucks baby-sitting."

Later that morning, Jessi and Mal and I walked Sonny to the address that Laine had given us. (Stacey and Mary Anne were taking care of Rowena and Alistaire *again;* Claud and Laine had gone shopping; and Dawn had said, rather mysteriously, that she might leave the apartment, but she hadn't said where she'd go.)

"Thanks for coming with me," I said to Jessi and Mal. "I appreciate it."

"No problem," Mallory replied. "Sonny's our roommate. I feel like he's a member of the Baby-sitters Club."

"Yeah," agreed Jessi. "And now that I don't have to make a fool out of myself when we leave the building, taking Sonny out is a lot easier."

We found the clinic without any trouble, I gave my name to the guy at the reception desk, and then we sat down to wait with Sonny. I looked around the room. Most of the other people were also waiting with dogs. A few were whispering to cats in carriers. One man was holding a box on his lap.

"What do you suppose is in that box?" I asked softly.

"I hope it's something gentle, like a rabbit," Mal replied.

"As opposed to what?" asked Jessi.

"As opposed to a snake."

We never did find out what was in the box,

though. The man's name was called, and soon after that, my name was called. Jessi and Mal and I led Sonny back to a small room behind the receptionist's desk. A very nice doctor introduced herself to us. Then she gave Sonny a thorough exam.

"He seems perfectly healthy to me," said Dr. Tierny.

I breathed a sigh of relief. "Do you have any idea how old he is?"

Dr. Tierny looked at Sonny's teeth again. "This is just an estimate, but he's probably about three years old."

"Okay. Thank you." I knew I would have an easier time finding a home for a young, healthy dog than for one that was old or ill. "Come on, Sonny Boy." I paid Dr. Tierny the ten dollars, (apologized), and walked out of the clinic with Sonny, Mal, and Jessi.

"Now what?" asked Mal as we stepped outside.

"First we take Sonny on a nice long walk," I replied. "Then we make a bunch of signs and stick them up all over the neighborhood. I guess we should place a short ad in one of the papers, too. We'll say we found a dog and we're looking for either his owner or a new home."

Kristy

Jessi and Mal and I walked Sonny all over the Upper West Side. When we brought him home, Mrs. Cummings offered to pay to put the ad in the newspaper, which was very generous of her, and Mal lettered a flier. It looked like this:

FOUND
in Central Park:
One small dog, part collie.
Approx. 3 years old. Healthy.
Are you his owner?
Can you give him a good home?
Call LJ 5-6470

I borrowed money from Jessi and Mal, and took the flier to the library. I made as many copies as I could afford. Then I tacked them up in Laine's neighborhood, and also in the park, near where I had found Sonny.

Later, back at the Cummingses', I kissed the top of Sonny's head. "Old boy," I said to him, even though he wasn't old, "I have exactly six and a half days to find you a home."

Chapter 16

Dawn

Sunday

Today I left the apartment again.

I left it big-time.

I was not surrounded by a protective group of friends. It was just me and Richie. The two of us against a city full of thieves and murderers. You know what? We traveled from one end of Manhattan to the other -- and nothing happened. Nothing except that I found out something I'd been suspecting. I like Richie a LOT.

Dawn

Sunday morning. As usual, I was alone in Mr. McGill's apartment. But for once, I did not care. Why not? Because Richie was coming over. And we were going to go out! I was not even very afraid. After all, I had survived eight nights by the fire escape. I had survived the subway. I had survived several trips with my friends. I had even survived being alone in a strange apartment with a creep ringing the doorbell. (So what if the creep turned out to be Richie? He was a stranger when he first came to the door.)

When Richie asked me if I wanted to spend Sunday with him "on the town," I said sure. I also said, "How are you going to spend a day on the town on crutches? That seems a bit difficult." I had said that the day before while Richie and I were sitting on his fire escape, eating apples. We had done a lot of talking on that fire escape over the past few days. (We were getting tan.)

"You'll see," was all Richie would reply. Then he added, "By the way, I'm going to be busy this afternoon, so I won't see you. I'll come over tomorrow morning around ten, okay?"

"Okay. That's fine."

Now it was 9:57 Sunday morning. Richie is punctual beyond all reason. When he said "around ten," I knew he meant ten on the nose. In fact, if my watch said anything besides ten o'clock when the doorbell rang, I would reset it.

"Nine-fifty-nine and fifty seconds," I murmured. I began a countdown. "Ten, nine, eight, seven, six, five, four, three, two, one . . ."

Ding-dong!

I just love punctual people.

I checked through the peephole, then unlocked the door. "Hey!" I exclaimed as Richie entered the apartment. "Where are your crutches?"

"Gone," he replied proudly. "I went to the hospital yesterday afternoon. The doctor gave me a walking cast, see?" Richie held up his foot. Then he showed off his walking. "Doesn't hurt a bit," he added.

"Wow." I was impressed.

"Ready to do the town?"

"Just point me in the direction of the first sight," I replied.

Richie aimed me out the door. When we were on the street, we hailed a cab. "Madison and Sixtieth Street, please," said Richie.

"What's there?" I asked.

Richie shrugged and smiled. He wasn't going to tell me.

When the driver stopped at the intersection Richie had requested, I climbed out of the cab and looked around. I raised my eyebrows at Richie.

"Here we are," he said.

"Where?"

"Right here. On Madison Avenue. One of the finest shopping streets in the city. Here you will find Laura Ashley clothes, cowboy boots, boutiques, and bookstores. It's the soup to nuts of the shopping world."

"Thank you, Mr. Tour Guide," I said.

We walked around until Richie's ankle began to ache. (I bought a booklet of New York postcards to send to Jeff in California.) Then we took a bus uptown and walked a short distance to the Metropolitan Museum of Art.

"Look at this," said Richie, pointing. "I love this sight."

We were standing before the stately stone steps to the museum entrance. Above us hung large, colorful flags announcing special exhibits. Richie and I walked slowly up the stairs and stepped into a great, hushed hall.

"How much does it cost to get in?" I whispered.

Richie pointed to a sign. I think it said, "Pay what you wish, but you must pay something." That was nice. You could pay whatever you could afford.

We walked around for awhile, but a museum was really not the best place for Richie. Too much standing. So we left and ambled down Fifth Avenue. On our right was Central Park.

"Even I have been to the park," I said.

"Isn't it wonderful?" replied Richie. "A park right in the middle of this huge city. Eight hundred and forty acres of greenery." (I didn't mention it, but he sounded an awful lot like Mary Anne.)

When Richie grew tired, we grabbed another cab. "Grand Army Plaza, please," he said. We rode down Fifth Avenue until the park came to an abrupt end. The cab pulled over to the curb.

"Now where — " I started to ask.

Mr. Tour Guide cut me off. "The square before you is called Grand Army Plaza. Beyond that is the Plaza Hotel, the setting for the famed book *Eloise,* and also the place where, years ago, my father proposed to my mother. Down Fifth Avenue are more fine stores. Steuben, FAO Schwarz, the New York Public Library shop, Saks Fifth Avenue."

"Whoa."

"However, we will not be shopping in them. It's lunchtime." Richie led me to one of about a million vendors' carts that were blocking sidewalk traffic. "Two tacos, please," he said.

"Richie!" I whispered loudly. "I don't eat meat."

"Oh. Right. One vegetarian taco, one regular taco."

"Are you implying that I'm irregular?" I asked.

"I *hope* not."

The meatless taco turned out to be good. The shell was filled with lettuce, tomato, guacamole, and cheese. I ate the entire thing, trying not to think of all the warnings I'd heard about vendor's food.

"Now for dessert," said Richie.

We crossed the street and continued down Fifth Avenue until Richie stopped in front of a store called Godiva. The window was filled with boxes of . . .

"Chocolate?" I said, trying to hide my disappointment.

"Some of the best you'll ever taste."

"But I don't eat sweets."

"Okay. You don't have to eat a whole piece. Just *try* one. I promise you'll like it. I'll give the rest of the box to my mom."

Against my better judgment I found myself saying, "All right . . ."

Richie bought a tiny but very fancy gold-wrapped box of candy. When we left the store, he opened the box and handed me a chocolate. Claudia would have polished off the entire contents of the box before leaving the store. But I took Richie's offering and bit into it gingerly as if it might be a bomb. Mmm. The chocolate was fabulous. I finished the piece, but Richie didn't bug me to eat any more. He put the box away.

"It is now time to see Chelsea," said Richie, and we took another bus down Fifth Avenue to 23rd Street. When we got off, Richie turned right. We walked and walked . . . and walked.

"How's your ankle holding up?" I asked.

"Okay. It likes Chelsea."

We were no longer on 23rd Street, but we were still heading west (according to Richie). The blocks began to look different. I saw fewer and fewer tall apartment buildings and more and more houses. Well, that's what Richie called them. But they didn't look like houses to me. They looked like short apartment buildings. Many of them were brick, and they were connected in long rows, with a flight of steps leading from each front door down to the street. Patches of grass actually grew in front of some.

"If you like the grass, you should see the *backs* of these places," said Richie. "In the middle of the blocks are amazing gardens and terraces. People have planted trees and flowers. They can sit outside on their patios or porches. I'd trade our fire escape for a garden any day."

From Chelsea, we took a couple of subways and somehow wound up in a very different neighborhood that Richie called SoHo.

"SoHo?" I repeated. "That's a funny name."

"It stands for 'south of Houston Street,' " said Richie. (And by the way, he pronounced "Houston" the way it looks — house-tun — not like the big city in Texas.)

On Houston, we wandered in and out of art galleries and stores. One store, a clothing store, was overrun with actual live animals, which was weird, since it felt a little like a jungle to begin with. You'd thumb through a rack of safari outfits and find yourself facing a tree, a large parrot perched in its branches. And dogs and sleepy-looking cats roamed everywhere. Strange.

When Richie needed a rest, he said, "How about some cappuccino?"

"Sure," I replied, so we found a restaurant with small round tables set out on the sidewalk. We sipped our cappuccino and watched the world go by.

"It's sort of like eating at a cafe in Paris," I said, and Richie grinned.

By the end of the day, I was exhausted, and I thought Richie's foot was going to fall off. We had sampled Indian food at a tiny restaurant in the East Village. We had wandered through the maze of little streets in the West Village. (Once, Richie got lost.) We even took the subway to Chinatown. When I told Richie I'd already been there, he said, "Well, have you been to Little Italy?"

"No."

We walked, like, two blocks and found ourselves in a world of Italian restaurants. A street fair was in progress and Richie urged me to sample a cannoli, even though it was filled with sugar. Hard to believe that just a few blocks away were Chinese restaurants, egg rolls, pagoda-shaped phone booths. . . .

"What do you think of the city?" Richie asked when we were finally heading home, our stomachs stuffed.

"It's full of food," I replied.

Richie laughed. "No, really. What did you think?"

"It's amazing. I've never seen it this way."

"I know. You've seen Central Park, the Statue of Liberty, the Empire State Building, the World Trade Center, right?"

"Right," I agreed. "And those were fun experiences. But you're the best tour guide I've ever had."

I realized that I had not been scared once all day.

A Big Apple landmark -- the Empire State Building

Mary Anne

Monday

The weekend is over. The second half of our New York trip has begun. A week from today, we'll be back in Stoneybrook. (With any luck.) Incredible as it may seem, I, the New York addict, may actually be glad to return to Connecticut. Oh, I still love this great big city. I just don't love the man in the rain hat and sunglasses. I don't think there's any question he's following us. But I bet he won't

Mary Anne

follow us back to Connecticut. He sure was glued to Stacey and the kids and me at South Street Seaport today, though.

I had never been to South Street Seaport and I was dying to see it. It's an area in lower Manhattan that during the 1800s was known as the "Street of Ships." It was the shipping hub of the city, a busy place, swarming with seamen, merchants, and immigrants, and a harbor crowded with all kinds of sailing vessels. Over the years, the seaport deteriorated, but it has now been restored and is an area of museums, restaurants, and shops contained in waterfront buildings from the 19th century. There are things to see: street performers and fabulous ships, as well as plenty of special events such as fireworks. You can go to the seaport to eat and shop, or you can go there to discover history.

Discovering history was what I had in mind when I suggested to Stacey that we take Alistaire and Rowena to South Street Seaport on Monday. Stacey thought that was a great idea. (Even she had only been there a couple of times, and she wanted to go back.) Then the rest of our friends decided that they wanted to come with us. Mal and Claudia couldn't, though, because of their art classes.

"I wish Mr. Clarke would let me go with you and sketch ships, but we're probably going to have to do something like draw a statue for eight hours," said Claudia grumpily.

"Oh, chilly!" exclaimed Mallory.

Claudia glared at her so fiercely I thought flames would shoot from her eyes.

Anyway, in the end, Stacey and I, Alistaire and Rowena, and Kristy, Laine, Jessi, and Dawn traveled downtown to the seaport.

"Cool!" I cried as we stood on Fulton Street and looked around. We could have been transported to another century — except that the people were wearing blue jeans or leggings, black cowboy boots, silly T-shirts, and these green foam Statue of Liberty souvenir headdresses. On one side of us was Schermerhorn Row, an old-looking building with tall chimneys and lots of windows. Across from it stood the Fulton Market Building.

"Hey, a craft collection!" said Laine.

"A Laura Ashley store!" said Dawn.

"The Athlete's Foot!" said Kristy.

"The Body Shop!" said Jessi.

"World of Nintendo!" shrieked Alistaire.

"I wonder where Benetton is," said Stacey.

"Isn't there a toy store?" asked Rowena.

"Oh, no. It's the guy in the hat," I whispered to Stacey.

"What?"

"*Shhh!* Don't scare anyone."

"Well, where is he?"

"He's right over there by . . . Well, he *was* right next to that trash can."

"Are you sure?"

"Positive."

Stacey looked worried. But finally she just said, "He's gone now. Let's try to have fun. I wonder if we can find a toy store for Rowena."

"We should really go to the museums," I said. "Expose the kids to some New York culture. Look. This pamphlet says there's a Museum Gallery here, something called the Small Craft Collection, oh, and a Children's Center. Let's go there first. We can take Rowena to FAO Schwarz any day. And we do not need to go into every store. There are stores all over New York. Not to mention the rest of the country."

Too late. Half of our group was heading into Schermerhorn Row, which is full of shops.

And Alistaire was pulling at my arm, crying, "Oh, brilliant! There's a place called Sweet's!"

"It must *have* sweets then," said Rowena. "Lots of them."

"You guys, this isn't exactly what I had in mind," I was saying, when Stacey suddenly elbowed me.

"There he is again!"

This time we both saw him. He was disappearing into a crowd of people.

"All right. We have to do something," I said.

"I'll handle this," Stacey replied. "Hey!" she called. "Laine! Jessi! Everyone! We're going to take the kids to the Children's Center. Let's meet back here in an hour. Then we can have lunch."

Laine waved to Stacey. "Okay!" she called.

"What are you up to?" I asked her. Then, before she could answer, I exclaimed, "Oh, my gosh! I just realized something. Have you — "

"The kids are listening," Stacey hissed.

"Buy them ice cream," I replied.

So we walked until we found a place called Minter's Ice Cream. We bought Rowena and Alistaire each a scoop in a cup. (Cones were too messy, considering the kids were not dressed in anything even approaching play clothes.) Then Rowena and Alistaire busied themselves with their treats while Stacey and I held a whispered conversation.

"Okay," I began. "Have you noticed that we only see the guy when we're with Rowena and Alistaire? I mean, did you notice him when we went to Chinatown? Or any time we've gone out to dinner with your dad?"

"No . . ." Stacey answered.

"So obviously he's not after us. He's after the children."

"Or maybe," said Stacey, "just *one* of the children."

"Right. It would be easier to kidnap one child than two."

"That's not what I mean. I was thinking," Stacey said slowly, "that maybe this guy was on the plane from England with the Harringtons. And maybe — you know, like in those spy movies — he needed to smuggle a roll of microfilm to the United States, so he dropped it into Alistaire's backpack or Rowena's tote bag or something. And now he has to get it back, so he's following the kids, waiting for just the right moment to snatch one of them and get back the microfilm — or maybe the diamonds."

"Stacey, you sound like me!" I exclaimed.

"Well, it's no wonder. You made me start thinking like this. And it is weird that the guy turns up everywhere."

We paused.

We watched Alistaire and Rowena, who were stirring their ice cream into vanilla soup, and giggling.

Then I said, "All right. If that man really is after one of the children, then we ought to find out *which* one."

"Okay."

"So I think we should each take a kid and split up. The guy won't be able to follow both of us. So we'll see who he *does* follow."

"Hey, good idea," said Stacey. "Okay, I'll take Alistaire, you take Rowena. Tell her you're going to look for a toy store. I'll tell Alistaire we're going to do something special at the Children's Center."

"Okay."

Stacey and I waited until the kids had finished their vanilla soup. Then we split up. "Meet you with the others in about half an hour," I said.

Stacey nodded. She and Alistaire went in

one direction, Rowena and I in another. I tried not to look too conspicuous about keeping my eyes open for the spy/kidnapper.

"Where's the toy shop?" asked Rowena.

"I'm not sure there is one," I answered honestly. "Let's just look around. There are a lot of shops to explore."

Rowena and I wandered everywhere, up and down streets — Beekman Street, Water Street, Front Street, John Street. We passed a boat-building shop, a museum shop, and the *Titanic* Memorial Lighthouse. Rowena kept her eyes peeled for a toy store. I kept my eyes peeled for the guy.

I saw him twice.

Okay, I thought. He's after Rowena. How sad. She's such a little girl.

"Ow!" Rowena cried suddenly. "Mary Anne! You're hurting me."

"Oh, Rowena. I'm sorry. I didn't mean to." (I'd been holding Rowena's hand in a grip so tight it would have put Arnold Schwarzenegger to shame. I was petrified that she'd be kidnapped, now that I knew who the spy wanted.)

I looked at my watch. It was time to meet up with my friends.

"Rowena," I said, "we have to go back."

"But we didn't find a toy store."

"I know. We'll go to FAO Schwarz soon. I promise. And I know you'll like it. It has more stuffed animals than I've ever seen. Some of them are bigger than you are!"

Rowena walked happily to our meeting place. (The thought of FAO Schwarz had satisfied her.) Stacey and Alistaire were waiting for us, but no one else had arrived yet.

"Stacey!" I cried, just as she cried, "Mary Anne!"

"What?" we both said. Then I added, "You go first."

"The guy is after Alistaire," she whispered to me. "I saw him three times."

"No way. He's after Rowena. *I* saw him *twice.*"

Stacey and I stared at each other. "What does this mean?" asked Stacey.

"I'm not sure. . . . He's twins? He's after you or me?"

"Well, I don't know about twins, but it's the kids he's after."

"Both of them, I guess." I wrung my hands. "We *have* to tell Mr. and Mrs. Harrington," I said firmly.

Stacey looked pained. "Here come Jessi and

Laine," she whispered. I knew she meant, "We'll talk about this later."

We didn't have many chances to talk that day, though. Either Rowena and Alistaire were around, or our friends were. But at one point, when the others had walked ahead of us, and Kristy was pointing out something to the kids, Stacey nudged me and said quietly, "We'll tell the Harringtons this afternoon."

"Okay." I nodded, swallowing hard.

Near four o'clock, Stacey and I were standing in the Harringtons' foyer, having returned safely with Alistaire and Rowena.

The housekeeper came to meet us. "Mr. and Mrs. Harrington aren't home yet," she said, "but they told me to give you a message. They'll be having some time off. They won't need you again until Friday morning."

I glanced at Stacey. All we could do was wait.

Claudia

Wensday

We whent on another feild trip today we whent to a place called the Cloisters. It was very intersting looking. I liked drawing there. But the best thing about the day wasn't the trip it was waht Mac said. We had a talk. He started it and it sure was intersting. Now Im glad I came to new York. It was all wirth it. By the way Malory and I are freinds again.

It was our seventh day of classes at Falny. I had learned to dread them. All Mr. Clarke ever said to me was, "Work slower," or, "Do it over." Once he might have smiled, but I wasn't sure. It could have been a grimace.

When Mal and I arrived in Mr. Clarke's class on Wednesday morning, he said, "All right. Today is our day at the Cloisters."

The Cloisters? Oh, right. The Cloisters. Mr. Clarke had mentioned the trip the day before, but somehow I had forgotten. Now I remembered. He had told us that the Cloisters, a branch of the Metropolitan Museum of Art, located in some place called Fort Tryon Park, features medieval art. Only it's not just a building where you go to stare at paintings and statues. I mean, it *is* a building, but Mr. Clarke said it's unusual. And it looks out on the Hudson River. (Plus, since it's in a park, you feel like you're in the country.) Here's what's in the museum: a collection of art, *plus* parts of medieval chapels and monasteries — real ones from Europe. The structures had been taken apart, the stones were shipped to the United States, and then the structures were *rebuilt*.

(In case you're wondering, *medieval* does not mean "halfway evil," like I used to think. It means "having to do with the Middle Ages," which were the years 1000 to 1400 in Europe. And a *cloister* is part of a monastery or convent, or the monastery or convent itself. Okay. Enough of this stuff. It's too much like school. If it didn't have to do with art, I would be bored, too.)

When our class had assembled, we gathered our sketch pads, our charcoals, and our lunches. Then we boarded a bus. It was a special bus to the Cloisters, and some other people were on it, but most of the passengers were us Falny students. And Mr. Clarke, of course.

Mr. Clarke sat with Mallory on the bus. They sat in the front. I sat in the back. Alone.

As soon as we reached the Cloisters, Mr. Clarke turned us loose. "Just go sketch," he said.

Goody, I thought. I'll stay out of his way. This looks like a big place. I ought to be able to avoid him.

My first hour was blissful. There seemed to be lots of places in New York that felt so un-New Yorkish you could imagine yourself in a different place, or even a different time. Mal felt that way about Chinatown. Kristy felt that way about Central Park.

And I felt that way about the Cloisters. It was, I think, the most peaceful place I have ever been in. So I settled down and began drawing. I found a part of a chapel that fascinated me. I began a series of quick sketches, one after the other. First I concentrated on angle, then perspective, then the texture of the stones. I was very excited.

I barely noticed when Mal sat down next to me. (I had settled myself on the floor.) In fact, I jumped when she said, "I will go crazy if we have to do this all day. How can you keep drawing and drawing, Claud?"

"It's in my blood," I said dryly.

"Oh." Mal looked hurt.

I went back to my drawings.

The next thing I knew, Mr. Clarke was saying, "Very nice."

He couldn't be talking to me.

I turned around. Nope. He was talking to Mallory. Of course. Then I remembered: *You have to escape him!*

I stood up quickly. But not quickly enough.

"Let me see, Claudia," said Mr. Clarke.

I closed my eyes briefly. Then I handed over my sketch pad.

One of my sketches from our trip to the Cloisters

Mr. Clarke looked at what I'd been working on. Then he flipped back a page — and another and another and another. . . .

"Claudia, what are you doing? Trying to set an Olympic sketching record? We're going to be here for hours. Would you *please* settle down and concentrate on *one* drawing? Just humor me for once."

I didn't bother to answer Mr. Clarke. I took back my sketch pad, turned to a fresh page, moved to a different spot, and started drawing again. I was so angry that I worked on one drawing for *three and a half hours*. I almost forgot to eat my lunch.

Mr. Clarke didn't say another word to me the entire time we were at the Cloisters. He walked by me twice and checked out my work, but then he just moved on. Good. I was sending silent signals to him. The signals warned, "Keep away. Don't talk to me. Keep away. Don't talk to me."

They must have been pretty strong.

When the time came for us Falny students to leave the Cloisters, I was exhausted. I don't think I had ever worked or concentrated so hard. I staggered onto the bus. I wasn't sure where Mal was, and I didn't care.

Halfway down the aisle, I saw her. She was

about to slide into the empty seat next to Mr. Clarke, but when he looked up and spotted me, he said, "Oh, excuse me, Mallory." He jumped up. "Claudia, I'd like to talk to you."

Oh, fabulous. This was just fabulous. What a way to end the day. I was only thirteen years old, and someone was going to tell me that my career as an artist was over — before it had even started.

I was an eighth-grade failure.

I wondered if there was a future in knowing the contents of every single Nancy Drew book ever written. That was my only other talent.

I plopped myself down in a seat next to the window. Mr. Clarke sat beside me. I waited for him to deliver the bad news and wondered if I could make it back to Stacey's before I began to cry.

"You worked very hard today," Mr. Clarke began.

Was this some kind of trick?

"Yes," I said cautiously.

"May I see what you worked on?"

As the doors to the bus closed and we eased out of the parking lot, I opened my pad and showed Mr. Clarke the three-and-a-half-hour drawing.

He looked at it for a long time. (During that

time, I thought, Nurse? Cab driver? Professional baby-sitter?) At last he said, "Now *this* is what I've been waiting for, Claudia."

"What?"

"I knew you could do it. I knew you could settle down, concentrate, and show some discipline. This is one of the finest pieces of work I've ever seen. And from such a young student, no less."

I must have looked completely confused, because Mr. Clarke went on, "I'm sorry I've been so hard on you, Claudia. I know you've been upset. But you are one of the most gifted artists I've had the pleasure of working with."

"Really?" Mr. Clarke sure had an odd way of letting people know he was pleased.

"Yes." He nodded. "You are also distractible and undisciplined."

"Oh." I paused. Then I asked, "Is Mallory Pike disciplined and — and — "

"Focused?" Mr. Clarke finished for me. He lowered his voice. "I suppose so. She certainly concentrates. And she tries very hard. But *you* are talented. However, to be a success, you have to be disciplined, too. Put you and Mallory together and we'd have one great artist. If you continue to work as you work now, your talent will go to waste. But you can develop discipline. Talent cannot be developed."

I thought about Mal. She wanted to learn to illustrate. She wanted to draw cute bunnies and mice. Maybe she could do that. But if I didn't concentrate and learn to become disciplined, I would not become an artist. Was that why Mac pushed me so hard? Because I had potential?

I checked it out. "You pushed me because I have potential?" I asked.

Mac nodded. "Great potential."

"Thank goodness. I didn't *really* want to be a cab driver."

"Excuse me?"

"Nothing."

The bus rolled on. We were in midtown Manhattan again.

"How much longer will you be attending my classes?" asked Mac.

"Just tomorrow. Then I go back to Connecticut."

"Do you have a good teacher there?"

"Not as good as you."

Mac smiled. "Thank you. Will you promise to study hard?"

"Yes." What else could I say? The one and only McKenzie "Mac" Clarke had just told me

I had enormous talent. I felt like throwing my arms around him, but of course I didn't.

A few minutes later, we filed off the bus.

"See you tomorrow!" I called to Mac. "Hey, Mal! Wait for me!"

I had to wait longer than I'd expected. Mal said she needed something from the classroom. She returned looking subdued. But as we rode back to Stacey's, I couldn't stop grinning. I knew that lots of hard work lay ahead of me, but so what? I could do anything.

"Claudia?" said Mal tentatively, as we flew along a side street. "I don't think this serious art stuff is really for me. I'm glad I tried it, but I'm going back to my animals and mushrooms and raindrops. My kind of art."

"Mal, I'm sorry," was my reply. (I meant for being so mean.)

She must have understood because she said simply, "That's okay."

Kristy

Wednesday

Today I woke up in a panic. (Or as Watson would say, in a tizzy.) It was Wednesday. I had exactly three days to find a home for Sonny. This was not a lot of time. What would happen if I awoke on Saturday and still had no home for Sonny? I couldn't bear to think of him all cramped up in a wire cage at a shelter or a pound. Sonny would hate that. And who would give him ice cream (his favorite treat)? Who would scratch those special spots behind his ears? I just had to find a home for Sonny. If I didn't, then I'd bring him back to Stoneybrook with me after all and hope for the best.

You'd think that with all the Sonny signs we'd put up, and that with the millions of people who must have walked by them everyday, I'd have received more than one call from someone wanting a dog.

That one call came on Monday evening. Laine's father answered the phone. Then he said, "Kristy, this man saw one of your signs. He wants to talk to you about Sonny. He sounds pretty interested."

"Oh!" I said. I wasn't sure whether to feel relieved or sad. I needed to find a good home for Sonny, but in the back of my mind I was hoping it would be at our house in Connecticut.

I took the phone from Mr. Cummings. "Hello?" I said.

"Hello?" answered a voice. "I'm calling about the collie. I saw a sign . . ." The voice trailed off.

"Is he *your* collie? Did you lose him?"

"No. I'm looking for a pet for my children."

"Well, Sonny is very good-natured," I assured the man. "He's gentle and he loves to play. And even though he's a stray, he's healthy. I took him to the vet. No mange or anything."

"How old is he?" asked the man.

"Three."

"Three months?"

"No, three years." *Sheesh.* I had put that on the sign. Didn't the guy read?

"Oh. Sorry. I guess I'm not interested then. I'm looking for a puppy for my kids."

"Okay." I hung up. Sonny was sitting beside me. I bent down to scratch the spots behind his ears. "You wouldn't have wanted to live with that family anyway," I told Sonny. "The father is an airhead."

By Wednesday, though, I almost wished that the airhead had decided to take Sonny. But only because no one else seemed to want him. The Cummingses liked Sonny all right, but they were serious about not getting a pet. Mr. McGill was interested in Sonny, but didn't see how he could care for him by himself. "Who would walk him while I'm at the office all day?" he asked.

Good point.

On Wednesday, in an attempt to un-tizzy myself, I decided to take Sonny for a walk in the park, just the two of us. I was clipping his leash to his collar when the phone rang.

"It's for you, Kristy!" called Laine's mom.

"Okay!" I looked at Sonny. "You wait right here," I told him. "When I come back, we'll take our walk. Maybe I'll buy you an ice cream." I ran to the kitchen, where Mrs. Cummings handed me the phone.

"Hello?" I said.

"Hello?" answered a small voice. It belonged to a child.

"Who is this?" I asked. I didn't think it was Karen or Andrew.

"This is Brandon."

"Brandon?"

"Mm-hmm. I saw your sign about the dog. I want one. Mommy and Daddy said I could have one. I'm nine years old. I'm very responsible."

I smiled. But then I remembered the other phone call. "The dog's name is Sonny," I told Brandon, "and he's three years old. He's not a puppy."

"Oh, good. So he's trained, right?"

"Right."

"Phew. Daddy doesn't want to have to train a dog. He says it's too much work. Especially in an apartment."

"I guess that's true."

"I've been wanting a dog for a long time," Brandon informed me.

"Well, would you like to meet Sonny?"

"Sure!"

"Great. When?"

"Right now. I want to meet him right now."

I hesitated. I'd been hoping that Brandon couldn't see him until the next day. Then I could spend a little more time with Sonny. I also knew that the sooner I met Brandon's family and saw their apartment, the better.

"Okay," I said to Brandon. "Where do you live?" (Maybe he lived in Minnesota. Or in a building that doesn't allow pets.)

Brandon gave me his address. He lived just four blocks from Laine. And, he said, practically everyone in his building had a pet.

Oh.

"Mrs. Cummings?" I called after I'd hung up the phone. "That was a little boy who wants to see Sonny. I'm going to walk him to Brandon's apartment." I gave Mrs. Cummings the address, and she said she'd come pick me up in an hour. I didn't know whether I wanted to be with or without Sonny then.

"Good luck," called Mrs. Cummings.

"Well, boy," I said as I walked Sonny down Laine's block, "you're going to meet someone named Brandon. He might be your new owner."

Sonny gave me a doggie smile.

"Be on your best behavior," I went on. "Mind your manners."

Sonny and I reached Brandon's block, which wasn't as fancy as Stacey's. The buildings were smaller, and some looked rundown. But Brandon's building seemed nice enough. I led Sonny up a flight of stairs and through a doorway. In the vestibule, I saw a panel of buttons. I pressed the one marked 3B — Leech.

An excited voice blared over the intercom. "Is that Kristy? And my dog?"

"Yup," I replied.

"Okay. Come on up. We're on the third floor."

Brandon buzzed the inner door for me, and I pushed it open. "Come on, Sonny," I said. The door closed behind us. I looked at the hallway. It was dark and shabby. Also, there was no elevator. "You're going to get a lot of exercise if you move here," I told Sonny.

We walked up two long flights of stairs. Sonny was huffing and panting by the time we reached the third floor. (So was I.)

I was beginning to peer at the numbers on the apartment doors, when one door flew open and a little boy bounded into the hall.

"Hi, I'm Brandon," he announced.

"I'm Kristy," I replied, "and this is Sonny."

Brandon knelt down. He looked seriously into Sonny's eyes. "Do you like to play ball?" he asked.

Sonny stretched forward and licked Brandon's nose.

Brandon laughed. "Come on inside," he said. He took Sonny's leash.

I followed Brandon and Sonny through the open door and into a small apartment. A man was standing in front of a couch. He stuck out his hand. "Hello," he said. "I'm Mr. Leech, Brandon's father."

I introduced myself, and then Mr. Leech told me about Brandon and his family. Mrs. Leech was at work, he said. (Mr. Leech worked at night.) Brandon had no brothers or sisters and was occasionally lonely. His father thought a gentle dog would be good for Brandon, and anyway, Brandon had been asking for a pet.

While Mr. Leech was talking, Brandon was patting Sonny and tossing a ball to him. I couldn't tell whether he'd been listening to his father. At any rate, he soon spoke up. "I promise, promise, promise I'll take extra good care of Sonny. I'll play with him and I'll remember to feed him and I'll walk him a lot. I won't forget to fill his water dish or anything. Honest."

I looked around the Leeches' apartment. It was small. The furniture was old and worn. But someone had crocheted afghans for the couch, and dried flowers were arranged in vases. Plus, Mr. Leech obviously cared very much for his son, while Brandon already cared for Sonny.

I smiled at Mr. Leech and then at Brandon. I knew I had found the right home for Sonny, Son of Louie.

"What are you going to call Sonny?" I asked.

"You mean I can *keep* him?" replied Brandon.

"If it's okay with your dad."

"He's all yours," Mr. Leech said to Brandon.

"All *right!*" cried Brandon. He threw his arms around his father, then around me, and finally around Sonny.

"So what are you going to call him?" I asked again.

I could barely hear Brandon's answer, since his face was still buried in Sonny's neck. But I think this is what he said:

"I'm going to call him Sonny, of course."

Mallory

Wednesday

Well, today was pretty interesting. In some ways it was sad, but in other ways it was... helpful. I can't exactly say it was happy or even good. Just helpful. I'm not upset. In fact, I've been doing some thinking, rearranging my thoughts. Oh, and I've got a great idea.

Mallory

Enough is enough. All right already. *¡Basta!* (That's Spanish for *enough,* I think.) If I had to draw another building or statue or cardboard box, my head would explode. It would not be a pretty sight. (Of course, I've never seen an exploded head, but I can't imagine that it would be a pretty sight.)

Wednesday was the next to last day of classes at Falny for Claudia and me. (No Friday classes, remember?) I went, but not because I particularly wanted to. I went because my parents had paid for two weeks of classes and because I liked Mac and didn't want to hurt his feelings by not showing up. Also, we were taking a field trip to this place called the Cloisters, and I was curious to see actual old buildings that had been shipped to the United States from Europe and rebuilt stone by stone.

We took a bus to the Cloisters. I sat with Mac. (Claudia sat in the back of the bus by herself, looking pouty.)

"Read any good books lately?" Mac asked me as the bus lurched through the city streets. He asked me that every day.

"I started a new one last night," I replied. "It's *really* good. But it's very sad. It's called

A Summer to Die, and it's about this girl whose older sister is dying of leukemia."

"Who's the author?" asked Mac. He had reached into his pocket and pulled out a notepad. He wrote down the title and then waited for my reply.

"Lois Lowry," I said. "She's written tons of good books. I bet your daughter would like them. She wrote the Anastasia books and *Find a Stranger, Say Good-Bye*, and . . ."

Mac and I talked about books all the way to the Cloisters. That was the fun part. The boring part was the rest of the day.

After I had looked around the museum and seen the ancient monasteries and stuff, I knew I had to start drawing.

I found Claudia.

I watched her for awhile as she sketched.

How does she do it? I wondered.

I asked Claudia about her work, but she was so grouchy.

I settled myself in front of the rebuilt corner of a stone building. I liked that corner. It was handsome. But I didn't feel like *drawing* it. How boring. I looked around. Mac was nearby. With a sigh, I began to sketch. A few minutes later, Mac was looking over my shoulder.

"Very nice," he said. He smiled and went on.

When he was out of sight, I looked for a long time at my drawing of the stone wall. It *was* nice. So I added some tufts of grass in front of it. Fuzzy little mounds of grass, the stalks waving in the breeze.

Then, next to a grass tuft, I drew a field mouse. It was a boy mouse, so I put a cap on his head. Then I erased the top of his body and gave him a baseball jacket. I decided he should wear glasses, like me. I added a pair of round spectacles.

Then I gave him a bat.

And a baseball.

This is Ryan Mouse, I told myself. He's a country mouse. And he's waiting for his girlfriend, who lives in a town. Her name is Kara Mouse. No, Angela Mouse. No, Meaghan Mouse. That's it. Meaghan Mouse.

I began Meaghan. I gave her a hip mouse outfit — a huge sweat shirt and leggings. But I had to erase the leggings. They were not meant for mouse legs. I gave her high-tops instead. And some jewelry.

Now, I thought, Ryan and Meaghan are going to have a picnic in the forest. Only — an evil gnome is after them.

Mallory

I drew an ugly, warty creature with fangs and claws.

And then I stopped drawing. I stared at my page.

I loved it.

But Mac would not like it.

I labeled the drawing Field Mice in Deep Trouble.

I really wanted to finish it, but I knew what I had to do. I returned to sketching the stuff in the Cloisters. I sketched for the rest of the day. I was bored to death. The highlight of the day was our lunch break.

At lunchtime, Mac and us Falny students took our food outside. I sat next to Claudia. What a terrific-looking lunch she had packed — a Fluffernut sandwich, Oreos, a couple of chocolate chip cookies, and some Fritos. It was not necessarily healthy, but it was tasty.

"How was your morning?" I asked Claud.

"Fine."

"Your lunch looks — "

"Hey, you're not my mother. There's nothing wrong with this lunch. Anyway, I packed apple juice. And there are raisins in the chocolate chip cookies," she added defensively.

"I wasn't going to . . . Oh, never mind."

Sometimes Claudia was not worth talking to these days. I stood up and left. I didn't see Claud again until we were boarding the bus to go back to Manhattan.

She sat with Mac!

I thought she didn't like him, but they talked during the entire bus ride.

And then a horrible thought occurred to me: Claudia was in trouble. Mac was telling her that her work was no good. I thought her work was great, but I'm no expert. Uh-oh. If Mac was telling Claudia that her career had reached a dead end, she would probably never speak to me again.

While Mac and Claudia talked, I twisted my hands nervously. I played with my hair. Life with Claudia was going to be torture.

But when we reached Falny, Claudia looked happy. No, she looked radiant. She was *beaming*. She smiled at me. And as we got off the bus, she actually spoke to me. I mean, spoke nicely.

"Mac and I just had the best talk!" she exclaimed.

"What were you talking about?"

"Oh, my art."

"Yeah?" I said hesitantly. "What did Mac say?"

Mallory

"Just that he thinks I'm" (I prepared myself to hear the worse) "very talented. He says my work is really good, especially for someone my age."

"He *did?* That's terrific!"

"He also said I have to concentrate on discipline and stuff, but I can live with that."

I nodded. I felt confused, though. Mac had been hounding Claudia since our first morning at Falny: "Do it over." "Work more slowly." And he had said that my drawings were "nice" or "good." But he had never said I was very talented or anything like that. What was going on? I needed to talk to Mac.

"Claud?" I said. "I — I forgot something in our classroom. I'll be right back."

I ran to our room at Falny and found Mac gathering up some sketches and putting them into a portfolio. "Mac?" I said.

He glanced up. "Mallory. I thought you'd gone home."

"Well, Claudia's waiting for me downstairs, but I have to ask you something."

"Yes?"

"Am I really a good artist?"

Mac stopped what he was doing. "You're dedicated," he replied. "Yes, you're good."

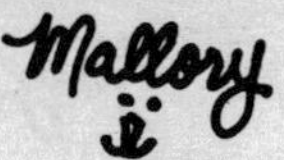

"But am I going to be a great artist one day? And have shows in galleries?"

"You're only eleven, Mallory. It's a little early to tell. But if you're asking me whether you have Claudia's talent, the answer is, I don't think so. If you keep drawing, though, I'm sure you'll become a better artist."

"Good enough to illustrate books?"

"Maybe."

I thought about my field mice, Ryan and Meaghan. I liked them a lot. I was sorry they were in Deep Trouble. Then I thought about the actual drawings of Ryan and Meaghan. I knew they were good. Good for dressed-up animals, anyway, and good for an eleven-year-old.

"Thank you, Mac," I said, turning to leave.

"Mallory, I'm sorry. I know you're disappointed."

"It's okay," I said.

And it really was. As I walked outside to meet Claudia, I thought, There are lots of different kinds of art, and I don't enjoy Claudia's kind or Mac's kind. I like my own kind. And I like writing even better.

I thought of Ryan and Meaghan again, only this time I imagined them in New York City.

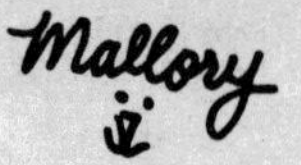

They went to the Museum of Natural History and scaled a brontosaurus skeleton. They snuck into Radio City Music Hall and watched all the shows for free.

By the time Claud and I were zooming back to Stacey's in a cab, I was writing a New York mouse story in my head. I was happy. I was excited. I had a terrific idea.

I planned to write a book soon.

Jessi

Thursday

I am in heaven. That's all I have to say.

Jessi

On Thursday, I saw Quint again. We went to another special performance of a ballet. This time we saw a production of *Coppélia,* which I have actually danced in myself. When the show was over, Quint said, "Want to get a soda or something?"

"Sure," I replied. (Anything to lengthen the afternoon.)

Quint walked me to a nearby coffee shop.

I ordered a diet soda.

Quint ordered a vanilla egg cream.

I changed my mind and ordered a vanilla egg cream, too.

In case you've never tasted one, an egg cream is a wonderful drink. It's made of soda and milk and either vanilla or chocolate syrup. (Surprisingly, it does not have any eggs in it.) I have never had one except when I've been in New York.

The egg creams arrived and Quint and I sipped them slowly.

Quint didn't say much. He looked thoughtful.

So I spoke up. "There are lots of good parts in *Coppélia* for guys," I said.

"I know."

Jessi

"If *you* went to a professional school, you could dance in *Coppélia.* I have."

"Yeah."

"Yeah what?"

"You know what, Jessi. It's everything we've already talked about."

"I want to hear you say it again."

Quint sighed. "Okay. I know I'm a good dancer."

"You're better than just good if your teachers think you can get into Juilliard."

"All right, I'm better than a good dancer. I would like to perform onstage in front of a big audience someday. Just like you have."

"So?"

"Come on, Jessi. You know all this stuff."

"Tell me again."

"I'm not going to audition because if I do get into Juilliard, I'll never be able to walk down my own street again. Not even with the bowling bag. I just don't think I can take all the comments and yelling and stuff."

"There are all kinds of prejudice, Quint," I said. "I've lived with it. You've lived with it. My friend Claudia has lived with it because she's not such a great student. Mallory gets teased because — "

Jessi

"I know what you're saying, Jessi."

"And you're going to deprive America of your talent because of a few jerks?"

Quint smiled. "Well, when you put it that way . . ."

"Do you *want* to go to Juilliard?" I asked.

"Yes, but — "

"So *go!* I mean, at least audition."

Quint stared into his egg cream for, like, an hour or something.

"Quint?" I finally said.

"I'm thinking."

After some more staring and thinking, Quint shifted his gaze to me. "You convinced me. I'll audition. If I get in, *then* I'll decide what to do?"

"You'll audition?" I screeched, forgetting where I was.

"*Shhh.* Yes."

"All *right!*"

"On one condition."

"What?" (I should have known there was a condition.)

"That you'll come home with me now while I talk to my parents. I'm not sure what *they're* going to think about this."

I thought I knew, but if Quint was worried,

then I would give him moral support. It was the least I could do.

Maybe someday I would be credited with having pushed the famous Quint Walter into the spotlight when he was afraid to go ahead with his career.

We walked back to Quint's apartment. We reached it just as his father was coming home from work. Quint and I glanced at each other.

"Dum, da-dum, dum," sang Quint softly. Then he said, "Hi, Dad. How was work? Did you have a good day? Can we have a talk?"

Mr. Walter put down his briefcase. "Hello yourself," he said to Quint. "Hi, Jessi." He kissed Mrs. Walter and was then tackled by Morgan and Tyler.

"How was the ballet?" Mrs. Walter asked Quint.

"Fine, but I really need to talk to you and Dad. I want Jessi here, too. But not . . . you know . . ." He gestured toward his brother and sister.

I'm sure Quint's parents thought we were going to tell them we wanted to get married, or something equally serious. They looked awfully worried. Maybe this was a good thing. Because when Quint said, "It's about my dance lessons," his parents lost around twenty pounds, just by letting their breath out.

"What about your dance lessons?" asked Mrs. Walter.

"I sort of want to take more."

"That's okay."

"They'll be expensive."

I was going to say, "Quint, you're avoiding the issue," when his father asked, "How many lessons each week?"

"A lot?" replied Quint.

I nudged him.

"What's going on?" asked Mr. Walter.

Quint looked helplessly at me, but I just looked back at him. I was not going to tell his parents about Juilliard *for* him. He had to do that himself.

"Go ahead," I said finally. "Tell them."

"Tell us what?" asked Mrs. Walter.

Quint gathered himself up. "I want to audition for Juilliard," he said. "I mean, if you can afford to send me there."

"Juilliard!" exclaimed Mr. and Mrs. Walter at the same time.

"Yes," said Quint. "My teachers think I can get in. So I'd like to try."

"All right," said Mr. Walter. "I think we can

manage it. Especially if you look into scholarships."

"All right?" repeated Quint. "You mean you don't care?"

"Of *course* we care," Mrs. Walter replied. "We're so proud of you. And if you got into Juilliard, well, just imagine."

"Besides, we're behind whatever you want to do," added Mr. Walter. "We'll stand behind Tyler and Morgan, too."

"That's not what I meant," mumbled Quint. "I'm glad you're behind me. And I'm glad you're proud of me. I really am. But do you realize what's going to happen if I go to dance school *every* day? Do you?"

"You'll develop huge muscles in your legs?" suggested Mr. Walter.

"Dad, this is serious!"

"Okay. I know some of the kids tease you. You have to decide whether you want to put up with that. Or else, you have to find a way to change things."

"Right," said Quint. He didn't smile. He stood up and stuck his hands in his pockets. He walked around the room. At last he came to a stop in front of me. "That's pretty much what Jessi said."

Jessi

"You're not worried about the audition at all, are you," I said.

"Nope."

"Just the kids?"

"Yup."

There was a moment of silence. Then the four of us began to laugh.

"Get through the audition first," said Mrs. Walter.

"Yes, Mom," Quint replied politely.

"Hey, Ma!" yelled Tyler from somewhere in the back of the apartment. "Can we come out now? We can hear you guys laughing."

Tyler and Morgan were allowed back in the living room.

I looked at my watch. "Oh! I have to go!" I exclaimed.

"I'll walk you home," said Quint. He turned to his family. "See you later. I'll be back soon."

Quint and I left the Walters' apartment. We stepped into the hallway. "Will I see you tomorrow?" I asked as we waited for the elevator. "I have to go back to Connecticut on Saturday morning."

"Saturday *morn*ing?" Quint looked dismayed. "I don't believe it. We're going to visit my grandparents tomorrow. We won't come home until Saturday afternoon. Or maybe even Sunday."

"That means we have to say good-bye now," I whispered.

"Yeah."

The elevator had not arrived yet. Quint and I were leaning against the wall, our shoulders touching. Slowly, Quint turned to face me. He took my hands in his. Then he tipped my chin up . . . and kissed me gently.

My first kiss.

"We'll keep in touch, won't we?" I asked.

"We better," Quint replied.

Stacey

Friday

Well, what a surprising day this was. I woke up knowing that Mary Anne and I would have to confront the Harringtons with the information about the guy who was following Rowena and Alistaire. After that, depending on whether we still had a job, we planned to take the kids to some of our favorite places, including FAO Schwarz, since Rowena still had not seen it.

The surprising thing didn't happen while we were wandering the city with the kids. It happened at the Harringtons' apartment in the morning.

Stacey

Our Friday outing with Alistaire and Rowena turned into quite an affair. First, Laine and the rest of my friends decided to come along with us. Mal and Claudia were finished with their art classes and, after all, it *was* our last day together in New York. This was not the morning surprise, though.

The morning surprise began when Mary Anne and I entered the Harringtons' apartment to pick up Alistaire and Rowena. (The two of us went by ourselves. We thought we would overwhelm the kids if all eight of us showed up. Also, we wanted Mr. and Mrs. Harrington's permission for our friends to spend the day with us.) As you might imagine, Mary Anne and I were pretty nervous. We had to have "the talk" with Alistaire and Rowena's parents. We knew we did. Rowena and Alistaire were being followed, and the Harringtons should be aware of it. What if the guy followed them back to England?

"Let's just hope Mr. and Mrs. Harrington are at home," I said to Mary Anne as we waited for someone to answer the doorbell.

"Do we *have* to hope?" asked Mary Anne. "*I* don't want to give them this news. It's too weird."

"We already decided," I said. "We're going to do it."

At that moment, the door was unlocked and opened.

In front of us stood Mr. Harrington.

"Hullo!" he said cheerfully.

I stiffened. Mary Anne took a step back.

Poor, poor Mr. Harrington, I thought. This could be his last happy moment. In a few seconds, he would find out that his beloved children were in mortal danger, being followed by a kidnapper, a dastardly criminal, possibly an international spy.

"Hi," I said in a small voice.

Mary Anne and I entered the apartment. We stood rigidly by the door.

"Well, now. What's on the docket for today?" asked Mr. Harrington.

Mary Anne just stood stock-still. So I answered, "Oh, a lot of things. But Mr. Harrington?"

"Yes?"

"Mary Anne and I need to talk to you about something."

"Is it your pay?" asked Mrs. Harrington. She bustled into the living room, fastening her earrings as she spoke.

"Oh, no," I said. "I mean, we do need to

be paid today, since we leave tomorrow, but the amount you mentioned is fine. See, it's . . . There's a little problem," I said, faltering, and wishing that Mary Anne would speak up. I knew she wouldn't, though.

"With the children?" asked Mr. Harrington, frowning.

"Well, yes — "

"Are they misbehaving?"

"Oh, no! They're wonderful. The problem is . . . well, it sounds sort of hard to believe. . . . I guess the best thing is just to come out and tell you." I paused. "Someone is following Rowena and Alistaire."

The Harringtons glanced at each other. I knew it. They thought I was crazy. If only Mary Anne would open her mouth, then they'd think she was crazy, too. I wouldn't be the only one. Oh, well. I'd started this and I had to finish it.

"It's a man," I went on. "We see him everywhere. But only when the children are with us. That's how we know he's following them and not us." (The Harringtons were smiling by this time, but I continued anyway.) "The guy wears sunglasses and a rain hat, no matter what the weather. He's never done a thing to the kids — he hasn't even come near them —

he's just always around. I know we should have told you about him sooner, and we were going to. Honest. But we weren't *sure* we were being followed, and we didn't want to accuse anyone of something awful like that if it might not be true." I was rushing on, talking like a record playing at fast speed. Frankly, I was blabbering. "Maybe we *should* have told you, but we just weren't sure. I'm sorry if we put the children in any danger, and I hope you aren't mad at us. See, it wasn't until Monday that we thought about the microfilm and the diamonds and the airplane and stuff. And we were going to tell you that afternoon, but you weren't home and you didn't need us again until today and I guess we could have called you but we didn't because we thought we should tell you in person so — "

"Stacey!" exclaimed Mrs. Harrington. Laughing, she held up one hand. "Slow down. You and Mary Anne didn't do anything wrong." She turned toward the hallway that led to the back of the apartment. "Bill?" she called.

Bill? Who was Bill?

This man walked into the living room. I had never seen him before. He must be an overnight guest, I thought. . . . Or a spy. Oh, no. Maybe the Harringtons were the *bad* guys. They were spies and this man was their agent and now the three of them were going to hold Mary Anne and me captive. Probably the housekeeper was in on the plot, too.

I looked at Mary Anne. She looked at me and shrugged.

"Don't you recognize him?" asked Mrs. Harrington.

Mary Anne shook her head.

I said, "Who? Bill? No. Should we recognize him?"

Mr. Harrington nodded to Bill, who nodded back, and left the room. When he returned, he was carrying a rain hat and a pair of dark glasses. He put them on.

"Aughhh!" screamed Mary Anne. "There's that guy!"

"Mary *Anne*, that's *Bill*," I said. I turned to the Harringtons and asked, "Who's Bill? I don't get it." And please don't kidnap us, I added silently.

"Bill is our bodyguard," replied Mr. Harrington.

"Your *body*guard?" said Mary Anne with a gasp.

"Yes. You girls were right in thinking that Rowena and Alistaire should be watched," Mr. Harrington continued. "It's unfortunate that they must be, but that's the state of our affairs. In England, we are very much in the public eye. And here in the United States, Mrs. Harrington and I are involved in international politics. We can't take chances. So Bill is the bodyguard for Alistaire and Rowena."

"Why — why didn't you tell us about him?" asked Mary Anne, who apparently was recovering from a great shock.

"Or why didn't the kids tell us about him?" I asked. "They know who Bill is, don't they? They must recognize him."

"Oh, they know Bill," replied Mrs. Harrington. "They know him all too well. And, they like him, but he makes them feel self-conscious. They're very aware of him when they're out in public. Having a bodyguard reminds them that they're in a different situation than most children are."

"So we thought we would try to give Rowena and Alistaire a *real* vacation," continued Mr. Harrington. "They know Bill is here with us, of course, but they don't know he's been following you around. And they *would* have recognized him, which is why he wore the hat and the glasses."

"But why didn't you tell *us* about Bill?" Mary Anne asked again.

"Because we thought you'd be nervous, that you'd overprotect the children, and we just wanted them to have a good time."

Mary Anne turned to Bill. "Will you be following us today?"

"Yes," replied Bill. He smiled. I could tell that he liked Alistaire and Rowena, which is why these thoughts began clicking along in my mind, and suddenly I cried, "Bill! Did you do something with the balloons that Alistaire and Rowena got at the street fair and then tied to the bike rack at the museum?"

Bill looked sheepish. "Well," he said, "I didn't want the children to be disappointed, and I knew they would be if they left the museum and found that their balloons had gone missing. So I checked on the balloons once, saw that they were gone, and ran back to the fair. I bought two more, but I think I got the wrong colors."

"One wrong color," said Mary Anne, laughing.

She looked as relieved as I felt. I began to

laugh, too, and was soon joined by the Harringtons and Bill.

"Hullo! You're here!" cried Rowena, running into the living room.

She was followed by Alistaire, calling, "Brilliant! Is it time to go?"

"Yup," I replied. "We planned a big day."

I asked the Harringtons if they minded if our friends came along, and they said it would be fine. So we set off.

" 'Bye, Bill!" called Rowena and Alistaire as the door closed behind us.

I think we walked about twenty miles that day. Our first stop (well, we took cabs there) was FAO Schwarz. Rowena said she could not wait one more moment to see it. "And," she added, "I *need* a toy."

"Well, you're in luck," I told her. "Your mother and father said that you and Alistaire could each buy one toy, as long as the toys aren't too expensive."

"They did? Brilliant!" exclaimed Rowena.

As soon as we entered the store, Rowena's eyes lit up. "Ohhh," was all she said.

And Alistaire whispered, "So many animals." (He meant stuffed ones.)

I thought for sure we were in trouble as we roamed the store and the kids kept examining things that were priced at hundreds or even thousands of dollars. But when Mary Anne finally said, "Okay, guys. What do you want to buy?" Alistaire chose a small stuffed dinosaur and Rowena chose a Skipper doll. Whew.

As we were leaving the store, I caught sight of Bill stepping off the escalator. I waved to him and he waved back. Then he straightened his rain hat and tried to look inconspicuous but official.

We wandered through Bloomingdale's. While Rowena sampled perfume, Bill hovered over a cosmetics counter, pretending to look interested in some lipstick.

We had lunch at the Hard Rock Cafe. It wasn't easy, but a waitress managed to seat the ten of us together. Bill sat by himself at a little table across the room. He looked pretty odd wearing his hat while he ate, and especially wearing his sunglasses, because the inside of the Hard Rock Cafe is on the dark side. A few people stared at him, but at least Alistaire and Rowena didn't recognize him. (I waved to him again. I couldn't help it.)

After a long day of shopping and sightsee-

Our favorite New York restaurant

ing, we returned the Harrington kids to their apartment. Mr. Harrington was home, and he gave Mary Anne and me our pay.

Then we said good-bye to Alistaire and Rowena.

And on our way out, we said good-bye to Bill, who was on his way in.

Claudia

Firday

Today was our last hole day in NY City. We spent most of it whith Roeena and Alistare but at night my freinds and I got to go out alone. We had an evning on the town and it was fantastik. Shoping, dinner in a restraunt and a show on broadway and we got to go by ourselvs accept for the guy who was driving the limmosin. I felt very special.

My friends and I (plus Laine) ended our vacation with a terrific evening. First we got all dressed up, and then Stacey, Dawn, and I went to the Cummingses' apartment. The eight of us looked like models or something. Even Kristy. She was wearing a *long* cotton sweater, black leggings, and black shoes. (She had borrowed everything from Laine.) The rest of us were wearing short skirts or dresses, leggings — you know, the layered look. A lot of our clothes were new, bought while we were on vacation.

"Where are you girls off to?" asked Mr. Cummings. As if he didn't know.

"Our night on the town," replied Laine.

Mr. Cummings clapped his hand to his head. "You know? I completely forgot!"

"Dad, you didn't. What about the limo?" cried Laine.

"Laine, I think he's kidding," I whispered.

"Are you kidding?" she asked.

"Of course," said Mr. Cummings. "The limo is waiting outside. It's at your disposal from now until the play is over. The driver knows he's supposed to bring you directly here from the theater."

"Okay."

In case you're wondering, Laine's father is a producer of Broadway plays. He's pretty well-known, according to Stacey. And he makes an awful lot of money, which is how the Cummingses can afford to live in the Dakota — and to hire a limo and chauffeur whenever they need one. (They don't own a car. Having a car in New York City is a gigantic pain.) Also, since Mr. Cummings produces plays, he gets lots of free tickets to shows. Our theater tickets that evening were free. If we'd had to pay for them, we wouldn't have been able to go. Most of us (especially Kristy) were pretty broke.

"Is it the same limo as last time?" I asked excitedly. (Once, during the time Dawn, Mary Anne, Kristy, and I had visited Stacey for a weekend when she was living here, Laine's father had hired another limo. It was incredibly chilly. When the driver hit the horn, instead of beeping, it played the first two lines from "Home on the Range.")

"The *exact* same limo?" said Mr. Cummings. "I doubt it."

Darn. Oh, well.

"You girls better get going," Mrs. Cummings spoke up. "You've planned an awfully busy evening."

That was true. We were going to look in a few of Laine's favorite stores before they closed for the day, then go to dinner at . . . Tavern on the Green. And then go to the show. Whew. (Chilly.)

We found the chauffeured limousine waiting in the street outside the entrance to the Dakota. Now, there are several sizes and kinds of limos. This particular one was a black stretch limo, which basically means it's large (well, long), and fancy. The last limo (the one that played "Home on the Range") was equipped with a TV set, a radio, a bar with ice cubes and sodas, and a partition between the driver and the passengers that you could raise just by pushing a button. I guessed that this was to give the driver some privacy.

"Oh, my gosh," said Mallory with a gasp, when she first saw the limo. "Look at that. When I get inside it, I'll feel like a movie star."

"Or royalty," whispered Jessi, whose eyes were shining.

Giggling, the eight of us crawled inside. (The chauffeur held the door open for us.) We settled down, the driver closed the door, and then he climbed into his seat.

" 'Scuse me," I said, since the driver's partition was down. I leaned over the front seat. "Does your horn play 'Home on the Range'?"

"Nope," answered the driver. "Sorry. It plays 'La Cucaracha.' "

"Oh, that'll do," I said. I sat down again.

The driver wound his way through the streets to this area of shops that Laine likes. He parked in front of a store called Mythology. "I'll wait here for you," he said.

I wanted to go in right away, but Laine stopped me. "We'll go in later. It's the best store, and I'm saving the best for the last."

So we browsed through a few stores. Finally I couldn't wait a second longer. "Mythology, puh-lease?" I begged. "I want to see those mirrors."

Laine knew what I meant, so we walked back to the store, and Laine led us inside and directly to a stack of boxes.

"Ah. The laughing mirror." I sighed. Then I held up the demonstration mirror, and just when I saw my face in it — the mirror laughed at me. "Ha, ha, ha, ha, ha, ha, ha." I began to giggle.

"Now there's a new kind of mirror," Laine

informed us. She held it up to Dawn's face, and the mirror screamed.

"Here's a fish flashlight!" cried Mary Anne. She squeezed the rubber sides of a pink fish, and a light shone out of its mouth.

We were all laughing. I think we could have stayed in Mythology forever, but Laine looked at her watch, drew in her breath, and exclaimed, "We have to leave! We're going to be late for dinner."

So I bought a screaming mirror, and everyone except Laine and Kristy bought fish flashlights, and then we made a dash for the limo.

"What is Tavern on the Green?" Kristy asked as the limo bumped along.

"Oh, it's amazing," replied Stacey. "It's this restaurant in Central Park, and the trees around it are lit with tiny gold lights. The food there is the best. Your stomach will die of happiness."

Stacey was right about everything. Plus, the people who ran the restaurant were really nice. I was afraid they might keel over when they saw eight girls and no parents walk in, but they just greeted Laine, and then a man showed us to our table. (It's nice to be known.)

"I think," said Mary Anne, looking around, "that this is the most elegant restaurant I have ever seen. In fact, you know, I bet it's not so much a restaurant as a fine dining experience."

I glanced at Stacey. We both hid smiles.

My friends and I opened our menus. I checked the dessert list first. Mmm . . . What a choice of food. All sorts of things were listed. I chose chicken.

So did everyone else. (It seemed safe.)

When dinner was over, it was on to the play. I climbed regally out of the limo, walked regally into the theater, paid regally for a large box of M&M's, slid regally into my seat, and then regally spilled the entire box of candy on the floor. One M&M (one M?) bounced onto this lady's shoe, and she didn't feel it, so it stayed there.

My friends and I became hysterical — only we didn't think we should laugh loudly in a Broadway theater, so we made our giggling worse by trying to fight it. Then, just before the curtain rose, Jessi said, "Hey, you guys, what's red and white on the outside and gray on the inside?" None of us could guess, so she said, "A can of Campbell's Cream of Elephant Soup."

Looking back, the joke wasn't all that funny. But on top of the spilled M&M's (one of which

Times Square -- on our way to the theater

was *still* sitting on that lady's shoe) it was hilarious. And periodically during the show one of us would think of either the candy or the elephant soup and laugh when absolutely nothing funny was happening.

I don't think we were very good audience members.

When the curtain closed about two hours later, we took one look at each other and started laughing *again*. We were still laughing when the limo stopped at the Dakota. But we did manage to thank the driver, who then thanked *us*, and hit the horn. As the car pulled into traffic we could hear a few bars of "La Cucaracha."

"I wish our car horn did that," said Kristy.

"I wish we didn't have to say good-bye right now," I said.

But we did. Stacey and Dawn and I were going back to Mr. McGill's apartment, and the next morning, Kristy, Mary Anne, Jessi, and Mal would bring their things over, and then we'd take cabs to Grand Central. So Dawn and Stacey and I wouldn't see Laine again for awhile.

I gave Laine a quick hug. "Thank you for *every*thing," I said. "These two weeks have been great. . . . I can't believe I rode in a limo.

Or that I have a mirror that screams when it sees me. Maybe I'll give it to my sister."

Then Dawn hugged Laine. "I had a terrific time."

"Really?"

"Yes, really. Well, after awhile I did."

At last, it was Stacey's turn to say good-bye. She and Laine threw their arms around each other. "I'll see you soon," said Stacey.

"I know."

"Come visit me in Stoneybrook."

"Okay."

Stacey turned away. She hailed a cab. She and Dawn and I slid inside.

I felt that our vacation had already ended.

Claudia

Well, we're back.

New York is a nice place to visit and Stoneybrook is a nice place to live. I guess what I'm trying to say is that I'm happy to be home, but I'm sorry our vacation is over. I think we all are, even Dawn. But I must say that our arrival at the Stoneybrook train station was pretty spectacular. Guess who came to meet us? Everyone in our families. They had all turned out when we left Stoneybrook, but when we returned, they were a little more organized. The Pike kids had made a banner on computer paper. They had printed out a picture of the Statue of Liberty at one end (obviously, their computer does graphics), then the words FROM NEW YORK TO STONEYBROOK, and then an outline of the state of Connecticut. Kristy's brothers and sisters and mom and stepfather were wearing blue

T-shirts with THOMAS printed on the fronts and BREWER printed on the backs. (I think Kristy was a little embarrassed by that. But when Emily presented her with her own shirt, Kristy nearly cried.)

I searched the crowd for my family. There they were. In the back. Not holding banners or wearing T-shirts. Just *there*.

I ran to them. I hugged all of them, including Janine.

"You're back!" said Dad. (Duh.)

"You made it home safely!" said Mom. (What did she expect?)

"Did you, by any chance, visit the IBM Gallery of Science and Art?" asked the genius. (Oh, my lord.)

"We did so much!" I exclaimed, deciding to ignore what they'd just said. "We went on a sightseeing tour — "

"On a bus?" asked Janine.

"No, a boat. We circled Manhattan. Did you know it's an island? And for art class we went to Rockefeller Center and the Cloisters."

"The Cloisters?" repeated my sister.

And for once, *I* was able to explain something to *her*.

Our big group of welcomers started to go home.

" 'Bye, Roomie!" I called to Stacey.

My other friends were calling back and forth to each other.

"See you tomorrow!" Mallory called to Jessi.

" 'Bye!" Jessi called back.

" 'Bye, Dawn!" I called.

" 'Bye, Mary Anne!" called Stacey.

" 'Bye, Claudia!" called Jessi.

" 'Bye, Stacey!" called Kristy. And then she added, "This is starting to sound like the end of *The Waltons*. " 'Bye, John Boy! 'Bye, Mama! 'Bye, Jim Bob!"

I piled my junk into the back of our car. There was quite a bit more than when I had left. I mean, you have to buy souvenirs and go shopping when you're in New York. Isn't that half the point of being there?

At home, I proudly showed my family the work I had done at Falny. If I do say so myself, my portfolio was impressive.

"Claudia, this work is so different from most of your drawings," exclaimed Mom.

"Do you like it?" I asked anxiously.

"It's wonderful," said Mom and Dad.

And Janine added, "It's totally, um, what's the word? Oh, yeah. It's totally awesome."

"I kept a diary, too," I said shyly. "Well,

sort of. I didn't write in it every day. But I have a good record of what we did. And my friends kept track of what they did. When they give me their notes and stuff, I'll make an illustrated trip diary."

Needless to say, Mom and Dad nearly keeled over with shock.

"What a wonderful idea," exclaimed Mom.

"I cannot wait to see the finished product," said Janine.

It took me a long time to finish my project. While I was working on it, the members of the BSC were keeping in touch with their New York friends. The mailman had his hands full for awhile:

Dear Mac,

I have ben working realy hard. I think you woud be prowd of me. I have ben working on a still life. It is some peices of fruite and a egg in a bowle near a vase of flowers. I have drawn it six times already. Mom says the egg will turn roten and begin to smell if I dont finish soon.

Sincerly,
Claudia

Claudia

Dear Mr. and Mrs. Cummings and Laine,

Thank you so much for letting me stay at your apartment. I had a great time in New York. Also, thank you for hiring the limo and giving us the free tickets and feeding us so many meals. How did you like having four extra daughters (and a temporary dog)?

I started my New York story. It is about Ryan and Meaghan, two field mice visiting the city. I want it to be very detailed and accurate. Do you happen to know how many bathrooms are in the Plaza Hotel? (If not, don't worry. I bet Mary Anne knows.)

Thanks again!

Yours truly,
Mallory

Dear Jessi,

Well, I did it. I auditioned. And I got in. Now I just have to decide whether to go.

Love,
Quint

Claudia

Dear Quint,
You better!
Love,
Jessi

Dear Jessi,
Okay, I did. Thank you.
Love,
Quint

DEAR DAWN,
THE DOCTOR IS GOING TO TAKE OFF MY CAST SOON. I CAN'T WAIT.
LOVE, RICHIE
P.S. THE FIRE ESCAPE SEEMS LONELY WITHOUT YOU.

Dear Brandon,
So, how's Sonny? I bet he's having a lot of fun with you. Are you giving him ice cream for a treat sometimes? I miss Sonny, even though my family has a dog, a cat, and two goldfish.
Give him a kiss and a pat for me.
Love,
Kristy

Claudia

Dear Kristy,

Sonny is fine. He is the best dog ever. We play in the park. Yes, I give him ice-cream. He also likes oatmeal. He can have all of mine. Thank you for my pet. I think Sonny misses you, too. (But not too much.)

Love,
Brandon

Dear Dad,

Hey, do you miss us?

Wondering in Connecticut

Dear Wondering,

Of course I miss you. I can't find anything. Ask Dawn if she knows where the salad plates are.

Love
Your Old Dad

Claudia

Deer Mary Ann and Stacy,
We are back in Englund. It is nice. I licked New Yurk. I rememberized the names of your freinds. Rowena licked the toy store.

Love,
Alistaire

my new york dairy is finished. I showed it to mom and dad and Janine. They thought it was grate. Mom even thought my speling had imporved but I am not so sure.

— Claudia Kishi

About the Author

Ann M. Martin is a former editor of books for children and was graduated from Smith College. Her other books include *Ma and Pa Dracula*; *Ten Kids, No Pets*; *Bummer Summer*; and all the books in the Baby-sitters Club series. She lives in New York, New York, with her cat, Mouse, and her new kitten, Rosie.

JOHN SIMPSON

About the Illustrator

Henry R. Martin is Ann's father, a well-known cartoonist who has written several cartoon collections and is published widely in *The New Yorker* magazine. He lives in Princeton, New Jersey, with his wife, Edie, and their two cats, B.J. and Pumpkin.

More titles... ➧

THE
BABY-SITTERS
CLUB